Find your power!

THE DEEP

Zetta Elliott

Rosetta
Press

The characters and events portrayed in this book are fictitious. Any similarity to real persons, living or dead, is coincidental and not intended by the author.

Printed in the United States of America

ISBN-10: 149290211X
ISBN-13: 9781492902119

for J'Cree,
who knows there's magic
everywhere

THE DEEP

BEFORE

1.

Come on. I want to show you something.

I'm not stupid. I know what it means when a boy whispers those words in your ear. But I was curious. And maybe a little bit proud. Proud that Trevor had chosen me—a girl who was only in eighth grade. And black—*real* black. Not one of those mixed chicks with blue eyes and barely tanned skin.

Besides, I'd fooled around with boys before. On my own terms, of course. I like to be the one calling the shots. Maybe that's what made Trevor so appealing. He wasn't used to taking orders from a girl. I figured I could teach him a thing or two.

Pride goes before a fall. That's what Gran used to say. I'm glad she's not here to see me now.

We met by the lockers half an hour before the dance was supposed to end. Trevor waited until the chaperones were looking the other way, then he took my hand and led me down the dim hallway. I told myself to play it cool. *Treat him like any other boy*. The door was locked but Trevor had a key. He unlocked the classroom and turned on the lights. I easily eluded his grabbing hands and went straight up to the board. I took a piece of chalk and started doodling, knowing that Trevor was watching me. Slightly amused. Mildly intrigued. Mostly impatient.

Let him wait.

"Want to play hangman?" I glanced over my shoulder and saw Trevor standing by the door, a mischievous grin on his face. I turned back to the board and drew a hasty gallows. I needed a provocative word. Then I heard Gran's voice and drew five blanks for the word Trevor would have to guess: L-Y-N-C-H. *In another time and place those boys would be lynched for chasing after all these white women.*

Whenever Gran used to talk like that, Daddy would just chuckle and say, "It's a new day, Mama. And this ain't the South. Besides, sisters are in short supply here in Germany." It's true—aside from those of us on base, there aren't many black folks in Kaiserslautern. To the locals we're strange and exotic, but Trevor was American—and white. Somehow that mattered to me.

I turned around and told Trevor to guess a letter. He made a sound that wasn't quite a laugh and said, "I know a game we can play that's a lot more fun." Then the lights went out.

That made my heart speed up a bit. With the door closed and the hallway lights dimmed, the classroom was pitch dark.

"Say something."

"Why?"

"How else am I going to find you?" he asked innocently. "Say my name." That was a command.

He couldn't see me rolling my eyes so I just said, "No."

Trevor took a few steps forward and banged into the sharp corner of a desk. "Ow—shit! Come on—help me out, Nyla."

"Not much of a soldier, are you? You'd be useless in battle." I silently moved across the front of the room, keeping the blackboard at my back. I stopped when I felt sure the teacher's wide desk was between us.

"Don't you want me to find you? You must be lonely way over there."

"Hardly."

There was a loud crash as Trevor knocked over a chair. He

cursed again and I laughed, then drew in my breath as I sensed him approaching. He'd found an aisle between the desks that led straight up to the board.

"Ready to play?" It was a question that sounded more like an order.

I should have stayed silent. I should have backed away from him and fumbled my way back to the door. But I went there to put that cocky boy in his place. I couldn't back down. So I took a deep breath and said, "Ready when you are."

His fingertips touched my bare arms. I shivered as his hands slid over my skin and found their way down to mine. Trevor held my hands gently and leaned in for a soft, tentative kiss. I relaxed a bit then, which was a mistake. Within seconds I fell into him and before I knew what he was doing, Trevor had my hands pinned behind my back. When I tried to tug them free he only tightened his grip. I knew I was in trouble then. Turned out Trevor *wasn't* like any other boy I'd been with before.

When I think back on it now, what I hate myself for most is the way I kept asking, how could this be happening to me? Trevor's free hand was up my shirt, inside my bra, digging past the waist of my skinny jeans. But instead of figuring out a way to break free I wasted time wondering if the attack—and my fear—was even real. Was he actually hurting me? Would he stop once he copped a feel? I couldn't understand how he knew how to do this. I shouldn't have cared. I shouldn't have tried to make it make sense.

I knew I should act—I needed to kick, scream, dig my teeth into his flesh. I knew I should do something but his mouth was all over mine. I couldn't see. I couldn't breathe. I tried to push back, press myself off the wall, but that only made him throw all his weight against me. I felt his hard-on and gagged at what was coming.

NO. That won't ever happen. Not to me. Not to me.

"Trevor?"

My eyes slammed open and searched for the dull blade of light cutting through the darkness. I groaned, tried to speak, but Trevor's tongue was choking me.

"Trevor!"

I gasped and sucked in air as his mouth finally tore away from mine.

"Get out of here!" he yelled over his shoulder. "Just get the fuck out!"

There was a pause, then I heard the angry flick of the light switch. The room exploded in fluorescent white glare.

"What are you guys doing in here?"

Trevor spun around to face down Allie's jealous, accusing stare. "What's it look like, stupid?"

Allie's green eyes traveled over our bodies but Trevor made no effort to zip up his pants. He just stood there leering at Allie, daring her to stay and watch him finish what she'd interrupted. Then Trevor laughed and his grasp on my wrists loosened just a bit, and suddenly my body did what it should have done five minutes ago. I reached for the desk and grabbed hold of the heaviest object I could find: a black metal three-hole punch.

Allie screamed as Trevor crumpled to the floor, blood spilling from the gash on his scalp. I wanted to swing again but I was frozen by the scream, the sound that should have come from *my* throat. So instead I dropped the three-hole punch and stood there watching Trevor's blond hair clot with warm, sticky blood.

I don't exactly remember what happened next. Someone must have called my parents because Cal and Sachi turned up before too long. Allie and I were in the school nurse's examining room. Trevor had been taken to the ER for stitches. Sachi ran to me and wrapped me in her arms. Then she felt me shivering so she pulled off her wool cardigan and tried to cover me somehow. My stepmother didn't ask what happened to the long-sleeve shirt I'd been wearing when I left the house earlier that night. She didn't say, "What were you thinking? How could you dress like that?" My father's accusing eyes asked those questions and more.

The principal came in and asked the nurse, Ms. Scholz, to wait outside. Cal listened to Mr. Weston's summary of events, then pressed his lips together and scrutinized me for a moment.

"Is that what happened, Nyla?"

I couldn't bring my eyes all the way up to my father's face. I stopped at the third button on his shirt. I didn't even bother to nod.

Sachi wrapped her arms more tightly around me. "Of course, it is. What's wrong with you, Cal?"

Cal didn't say anything else to me. He didn't even follow protocol. He went to the witness instead of the victim. "What happened here, Allison?"

Allie was a mess. I don't know why *she* was crying but all that mascara she wears to hide her blond eyelashes was running down her pale cheeks. She just sniffed and said, "Ask Nyla."

My father doesn't play that game. "Right now I'm asking *you*," he said sternly. "What did you see when you went into the classroom?"

"Nothing," Allie mumbled with her eyes on the ground. "It was too dark."

"Why did you go in there?"

Allie bit her lip. "I—I was looking for someone."

"Nyla?" Cal knew Allie and I weren't friends.

"N—no."

"You were looking for Trevor then." Allie nodded and flashed her bleary eyes at me. Expert interrogator Cal kept his eyes fixed on Allie. "Why did you think he'd be in that classroom?"

Good question, I thought to myself. And for the first time I realized Cal actually might be on my side.

Allie tugged at the silver fairy dangling from her right ear. "Because he wasn't in the gym. And..." Allie's voice grew quiet. "And that's where he usually goes."

Mr. Weston stepped forward, indignant. "That's impossible! All the classrooms were locked—I checked them myself before the dance began."

Cal kept his eyes glued to Allie. "Allison, do you know how Trevor got into that room?"

Allie shook her head too quickly to be believed. "I don't know!" She whimpered a bit but Cal showed no sign of sympathy. Allie bit down on her glittery pink lip and whispered, "I think he has a key."

Cal took a step back, giving Allie a bit of breathing room.

"I could hear...sounds. I could tell someone was in the room so I turned on the lights."

"And what did you see?"

"Her." Allie tossed me a vicious look. "And Trevor. They were all over each other."

Liar. I spat the word at her with my eyes.

"And what did you do then, Allison?"

"*I* didn't do anything. *She* freaked out."

"You saw Nyla attack Trevor?"

Allie looked up at my father and for a moment I thought his magnetic eyes would pull the truth out of her. But then Allie shifted her gaze and looked at the floor again. That made it easy for her to lie. She shrugged and said, "I don't know. I guess so."

Cal swung his eyes over to me. I wanted to be still and strong but I couldn't stop shaking. I told myself it was adrenaline, not fear. I let my body tremble but I kept my gaze steady so Cal knew I wouldn't back down or take back my words. I looked at my father but inside my eyes I was still seeing Trevor. *Touch me now, asshole. Just try to touch me* now.

"I want the truth young lady."

I blinked and realized that Cal was saying this to Allie, not me. He took Allie's chin between his thumb and forefinger and tilted her face toward his. For just a second I felt sorry for her. I'd been there before.

This time Allie couldn't look away. She stared into my father's grim face, then pressed her eyes shut as fresh tears streaked more black mascara down her freckled cheeks.

"They were—Trevor said…he told me to get out." Allie's voice caught in her throat and her shoulders start to heave. "I'm sorry. I didn't know he would—I thought he just wanted to…"

"Allie?"

"Mom!"

Mrs. Brooks rushed into the small office and practically smothered her daughter in a panicked embrace. Then Allie burst into loud sobs while her mother lit into the principal for being lax and letting students run wild at school.

Cal took pity on Mr. Weston and tried to reassure Mrs. Brooks. "Your daughter was very brave tonight. She quite likely prevented a criminal act from occurring on school grounds."

Mrs. Brooks stopped chewing out Mr. Weston and pushed Allie back so she could look her daughter in the face. "You did? But—how?"

She knew. Allie knew what Trevor was going to do to me. I never found out whether it happened to her too. Maybe some other girl walked in and saved Allie the way she saved me that night. Maybe not.

"We're going home, Cal." Sachi gently eased me off the examining table.

I flinched as my father pulled the cardigan up to cover my bare shoulder. "I can't leave yet—the SPs will probably have to conduct an investigation."

Sachi didn't bother to hide her irritation. My father is a true military man—rules and procedures mean a lot to him. "Then go do whatever it is you have to do," she snapped. "I'll take care of our child."

We walked home in silence. I took a long hot shower and let Sachi tuck me in for the first time in years. She sat by my bed, stroking my hand, until Cal came home. I couldn't sleep but I closed my eyes so my stepmother wouldn't feel she had to talk to me. What was there to say? When Sachi slipped out of my bedroom, I opened my eyes and crept over to the door so I could listen to my parents arguing in the next room.

"She didn't attack him, Cal. You know as well as I do that it was self-defense." Sachi was pacing back and forth. "Someone has to do something. Nyla can't be the only one. That little rapist knew what he was doing! How does a boy his age learn something like that?"

"Calm down, Sachi. We're going to handle this the right way."

Sachi's voice got louder. "The right way? You mean the way the military deals with soldiers who get raped? Because that's not the kind of justice I'm looking for, Cal. Not for our daughter. Not for *our* girl."

Cal sighed heavily. "I'll deal with it, Sachi. Just leave it with me."

"Leave it with you? This never would have happened if you'd listened to me. It's time to *go*, Cal. Your mother begged you to let her die back home—your own mother *begged* you! But I won't beg. I'm going, Cal, and Nyla's coming with me."

"She's my child, Sachi."

That was a low blow. When Gran had her first stroke, Sachi started talking about adopting me. If anything happened to my father, I'd be on my own—unless Sachi adopted me and became my legal guardian. Sachi's the only mother I've ever known really, but Cal wasn't ready to have that conversation. Cal's not ready for a lot of things when it comes to me.

"Well, she's *my* responsibility," Sachi said after taking a few seconds to recover. "You can stay if you want—wait for the wheels of justice to turn. They ought to crush that little bastard but he probably won't even get a slap on the wrist!"

"Nyla's got to take responsibility for her actions, too."

Sachi stopped pacing. Her voice got quiet, which is how I knew she was seriously pissed. "It was self-defense."

"He had it coming, I'm not saying he didn't. But she didn't hit him during the assault. She hit him after."

"Delayed reaction. She was in shock."

"In your opinion. You're her stepmother, Sachi. You're hardly impartial."

"I'm a medical professional and *I* say she was in shock."

"Unfortunately, Sachi, your professional opinion's not worth much on base these days."

Damn, Cal—another low blow. Sachi lost all her defiance then. I heard the springs creak as she sank onto the edge of their bed. "Just take us away from here, Cal," she said softly. "It's time to go home."

I heard my father sit down next to Sachi. "This is the only home Nyla's ever known. I'm not sure she could handle living in the States after all this time."

"Nyla can handle anything." There was a pause and I hoped my father was putting his arms around the woman who raised me as her own. "She doesn't belong here, Cal. That's the problem. She wants to, but she doesn't belong."

I closed my door and stopped listening at that point. *She wants to, but she doesn't belong*. Is that what made me follow Trevor into that classroom?

Gran used to live in a brownstone in Brooklyn but when my biological mother walked out on us ten years ago, Gran came to Germany to help Cal out. It was supposed to be temporary but Gran wound up staying until she had a second, massive stroke and died a few months ago. My dad hired a property manager to rent out the brownstone while Gran was over here. I wondered if that was where we were heading. New York City. Is that where I belonged?

I took the china urn that held Gran's remains off the shelf above my desk. Cradling it with one arm I crawled back into bed and wondered what Gran would say about everything that happened tonight. "What do you think, Gran?" I whispered to the ashes inside the cold urn. "Do I belong in Brooklyn?"

NOW

2.

Turns out I had to get glasses after all. Once Nuru returned to her realm last spring I started squinting at the board again. Nyla and Keem went with me to pick out the frames. I don't like wearing glasses but I don't really have much choice. All that squinting was giving me headaches and my foster mother, Mrs. Martin, doesn't need one more kid to worry about. She's already got her hands full with Mercy.

Nyla says my glasses' thick black frames make me look cool—"geek chic" is what she calls it. Nyla says people on the outside are really *avant-garde*—cutting edge. She says people on the inside look to outsiders like us to lead the way because they're too scared to leave "the herd." Nyla's got a theory for everything and everyone—geeks, freaks, and bullies. I'm kind of an expert myself, not that anybody messes with me now that I've got Nyla and Keem. But come September all that will change. Nyla's one of the few black students to get into Stuyvesant so she'll be in Manhattan most of the time. Keem's going to play ball at Boys & Girls. He'll still be in Brooklyn but he won't have time to look out for a middle schooler like me.

If they do have any spare time they'll probably want to spend it with each other. Nyla and Keem are…together. I don't know if they're officially girlfriend and boyfriend but I can tell they're really into each other. *Most* of the time. The rest of the time…I don't know.

School's out for the summer but I've been getting a real education in romance just by watching those two. One day they act like they're best friends and the next day they're going at each other like cats and dogs. Actually, when they do argue it's mostly one-sided. Keem's got to be the most patient guy I know—he almost never loses his cool. But Nyla? It's like she's testing him, waiting for him to walk away. And sometimes he does—but Keem always comes back.

Nyla's smart, pretty, and a lot of fun to be around, but people who don't know her might find her kind of intimidating. Nyla's edgy in both senses of the word—she's definitely avant-garde but she can also be touchy about certain stuff. Everything will be fine between the three of us and then all of a sudden something will set Nyla off. I've learned to just keep my head down and keep my mouth shut. But Keem—he's so desperate to be with her that he won't let Nyla push him away.

I understand. I used to have a crush on Nyla too, but these days I feel more like her little brother. Or if Nyla and Keem are arguing, then I feel like I'm their kid and they're my parents. I don't know what happened between my real parents. I guess they were in love once but something must have changed after I was born because my dad left and Mom didn't want him back. Maybe he left because of me. Nyla's says that's crazy—what parent wouldn't want a math whiz like me for a son? She says that's just how love is—it's not meant to last forever. Her mom walked out on her, too. Nyla says it doesn't bother her but I think she just doesn't let it show.

Before Nuru left, she told me to keep my heart open. I try but it sure feels a whole lot safer to just keep my distance from other folks. Keem, Nyla, and I have been through a lot—they risked their lives for me last spring and I'd do the same for them. I don't know what will happen when school starts in September, but deep down I hope our friendship will last. Keem's a star athlete so everybody wants to get next to him—especially girls. Nyla was the most popular student at our magnet school. She's got an entourage of "freaks" and even the cool kids show her respect. Me? I've got nobody really. Mrs. Martin took me in after my mom passed away last year. Then Nuru chose me for her host but in the end, she left me too.

Sometimes I look at Mercy and I think she's lucky to have been born that way. I mean, it's messed up that her mother took drugs while she was pregnant, but all those chemicals left Mercy with this invisible wall to protect her. In the beginning her nerves were so sensitive that it hurt for her to be held, even by someone as gentle as Mrs. Martin. Then she got so she wanted to be held all the time, but only by certain people. If Mrs. Martin's busy, Mercy will let me hold her for a little while. But if a stranger tries to pick her up, Mercy starts to wail. And there's something about the way she cries that makes you feel like the worst person in the world.

For a long time Nyla wouldn't go near Mercy. She said all her piercings freaked little kids out and Mercy would probably scream at the sight of her. I could tell Mrs. Martin was worried about that too, though she was too polite to say anything. My foster mother is an elderly white woman—she doesn't know *what* to make of Nyla. No one does. Nyla keeps everyone guessing. She looks like a rebel with her shaved head and combat boots, but Nyla's a straight-A student and her folks are actually pretty strict. They met in the military and that's why Nyla grew up on a base in Germany. Nyla's one of a kind and she says she likes being different but I know from experience just how lonely being different can be.

One day we were hanging out in the kitchen when Mercy started to fret. That's what Mrs. Martin calls the fussy noises the baby makes before she really starts to bawl. The baby monitor was on the counter but Mrs. Martin couldn't hear it since she was in the basement doing laundry. Keem and Nyla looked at me.

"You better go up there," Nyla said with a smirk.

I took another homemade chocolate chip cookie from the plate

Mrs. Martin had set in the center of the table. "Sometimes she goes back to sleep," I said, not wanting to go all the way upstairs. But within a few seconds Mercy's fretting turned to whining.

Keem nudged me and nodded toward the stairs. "Go on, D. Your little sister needs you."

Keem's actually really good with kids—he's the youngest in his family but I've seen him with his little cousins. They climb up his legs like he's a living tree, and then Keem tosses them up in the air until they're shrieking with glee. I wanted to suggest that *he* go up and check on Mercy but I knew it was my responsibility. When I got upstairs I could hear Nyla and Keem laughing through the intercom. "I can hear you guys," I said loudly, which only made them laugh even more.

Mercy stopped whimpering as soon as I picked her up, but by the time I carried her downstairs to the kitchen, Nyla was alone. She got up from the table and jammed her hands into the back pockets of her black skinny jeans. "Keem's helping Mrs. Martin," Nyla said, glancing nervously at the open basement door.

I was holding the baby over my shoulder but when she heard Nyla's voice she got curious and turned her head around. Nyla backed up against the kitchen counter and braced herself for the scream. But Mercy didn't start to cry. She just stared at Nyla with wide eyes and her little mouth hanging open. Then Keem and Mrs. Martin came up from the basement with two baskets of laundry. The kitchen's pretty small and so Nyla had no choice but to move closer to me and the baby. That's the only time I've ever seen anything like fear in Nyla's face.

Mercy usually lights up when she sees Mrs. Martin but on that day she only had eyes for Nyla. When she realized Mercy wasn't afraid of her, Nyla pushed her bangs out of her face and smiled awkwardly at the baby. Mercy's eyes widened when she saw the silver ball that sits just below Nyla's bottom lip. Mercy reached for it and squirmed so much that I finally had to hand her over. "Here, you take her," I said.

Nyla reluctantly pulled her hands out of her pockets and reached for Mercy. The baby happily sank into her arms and immediately started pressing the diamond stud in Nyla's nose. Then she reached for Nyla's silky black bangs. Mercy tapped the thick black plugs that fill Nyla's earlobes all the while making soft sounds of awe. Nyla held the baby close and whispered words I couldn't quite hear. Maybe she was speaking German.

Mrs. Martin watched Mercy, amazed. Finally she said, "Well, I'd better put this laundry away."

Keem just stood there mesmerized. He was staring at Nyla and Mercy like he was seeing his future family. But then Keem saw Mrs. Martin struggling with the laundry baskets so he offered to help carry them upstairs. That left me, Nyla, and Mercy alone in the kitchen once more.

I sat down at the table and grabbed another cookie off the plate. "She likes you," I said and then felt stupid for stating the obvious. But Nyla didn't seem to hear me. She was too absorbed in the baby. I shifted my chair a bit and leaned in so I could hear what Nyla was whispering into Mercy's tiny ear. It sounded like, "Stay strong, baby girl. Stay strong."

"Don't worry," I said, trying to reassure her. "Mercy's a fighter. She'll be alright."

Nyla didn't even look at me. She just pressed her lips against Mercy's soft baby cheek and then turned away so I wouldn't see that her face was wet with tears.

3.

For a long time nothing happened.

Last spring Keem and I thought we'd lost D forever, but Nuru sent him back to us in the end. Since then we've pretty much been inseparable. Keem and I—we're older and I guess we feel responsible for D. I'm not sure why. He may not look it, but D's a tough kid and he's already proven that he's a survivor. He found Nuru in the park just a few months after his mom died of cancer. D was lonely, the bird needed help…he couldn't have known how it would all turn out. None of us could.

Turned out the injured bird wasn't a bird at all—it was Nuru, a life force from another realm. She chose D as her host because she thought he had nothing to lose, but once D started to care about me and Keem, things got complicated. After we helped Nuru fulfill her mission she released D from service. He needed us more than ever after that. D misses her. I know he does. Life now is just ordinary. And who wants to be ordinary?

There are lots of ways to be different. Before I left Germany I got my first piercing—a diamond stud in my left nostril. Cal pitched a fit but what could he do? The next day Sachi and I boarded a plane and we didn't see my father for a couple of months. Those first few weeks in Brooklyn were hectic. The upstairs tenants hadn't moved out yet and the downstairs apartment was totally empty. Sachi couldn't buy anything so Cal had to order stuff for us online or else we had to do without. He could have just wired me some money but Cal's not that kind of father. My stepmother has a gambling problem. She ran up all her credit cards and blew through my college savings fund before we figured out what was going on. Sachi's a nurse but she lost her privileges at the dispensary because my father reported her as a potential risk. He thought she might steal painkillers and sell them to support her addiction to online poker.

Everyone acts like we left Germany for my sake but I think Sachi wanted a new start too. Even Cal probably wanted to be someplace where nobody knew about our past. Image means a lot to my father. He thinks the choices *we* make—good or bad—reflect *his* ability to run a tight ship. So Cal wasn't too pleased when he finally reached New York and found I'd pierced my lip, my ears, and my right eyebrow. I still had long hair then so most of my piercings weren't that visible. But that didn't stop Cal from freaking out, and that just made me want to go even farther. I added plugs to my earlobes and I shaved off most of my hair. What little was left I dyed wine red. By the time I met D and Keem last March I was done trying to prove my point. My body is *my own, my own, my own*.

That's a line from this poem I found on the internet—"Poem About My Rights" by June Jordan. It's really long but it's brilliant and she keeps asking, "Who in the hell set things up like this?" That's easy—men. You don't even want to *know* what comes up when you Google "rape." This world is a sick, sick place. But I knew I wasn't the only one. I knew Trevor had done to other girls what he did to me that night. I didn't want to advertise the fact, but I did want to talk to somebody. Problem was, I hadn't met many people in Brooklyn at that point so I went online instead. Sachi wanted me to see a therapist. She joined a group—Gamblers Anonymous—to help her deal with her addiction because she wants Cal to trust her again. I have a different problem—I want to be able to trust myself.

Sachi and I did take a self-defense class together once we got settled in. The instructor told us to honor our inner voice and avoid high-risk situations. But mostly what you need to do is make a lot of noise. I learned that rape is about control and the rapist expects his victim to be too scared to speak, never mind cry for help. It was kind of weird at first, being in a room full of strangers, all of us yelling at the top of our lungs. Then it was sort of fun—it felt like we were breaking the rules by making so much noise. And then—when we all yelled "NO!" together at once—it felt really amazing. I felt so strong—like I was unstoppable. I almost believed it could never happen to me again. Almost.

Cal and Sachi gave me a Swiss army knife for my tenth birthday and I keep it with me all the time now. I know which parts of the male body are most vulnerable—eyes, windpipe, groin. But I don't know what I could do against a gun. A few weeks ago this guy in Norway set off a bomb and then went on a shooting spree, killing seventy-seven people—mostly kids my age. Columbine, Virginia Tech, Tucson—women don't shoot up their classmates or their coworkers or the club. The perps are always men. But nobody talks about that.

When I was growing up on base, Gran used to get on me all the time about acting more like a lady. She always said I was "too wild" for a girl, and that when she was my age she wore a starched skirt every day and had to sit like she was holding an aspirin between her knees. But look at how guys sit—one knee pointing east and the other pointing west, taking up two seats on the subway and then copping attitude when you ask them to move over so you can sit down too.

I guess I should be glad that no one throws acid in my face just because I want to get an education. Lots of girls in other countries want to learn, too, but that's hard to do when some prick's burned down your school. Whenever I start to feel like men are ruining the world, I make a list of all the good guys I know. Not that I know him personally, but I usually start with President Obama. Next on the list is Cal. My father and I don't get along all the time but deep down I know he's a good guy, too. Ramstein was full of men like Cal—responsible, disciplined, hardworking. Not that the military doesn't have its issues. And it's messed up that we need men with guns to take down the psycho men with guns. Who in the hell set things up like this? Not me, that's for damn sure. Whoever thinks girls run the world needs to have their head examined.

I don't hate men—some of my closest friends are guys. I know that makes me sound like those racists who say, "One of my best friends is black!" But it's true. Before I met Keem and D I spent most of my time with Jamal and Darnell—they're both near the top of my List of Good Guys. Jamal's a scrawny skater geek and Darnell came out last summer, so they both know how it feels to be on the outside. Jamal's the one who introduced me to Sade. She and I used to be tight but these days we hardly speak. It's mostly because of Keem. Sade thinks I sold out by falling for a jock. But it's not like that because I haven't fallen for Keem.

Sure, he's good-looking—*really* good-looking—and smart, too. His family and his faith are important to him, and Keem's got more than just hoop dreams in that big head of his. And I'd be lying if I said it didn't feel good to see the gum fall out the mouths of those heifers at school when they saw Keem talking to me. Truth is, I feel sorry for those girls. They just follow the herd, thinking that'll get them a guy like Keem. I see them online, posting naked photos of themselves and then calling other girls sluts when guys post videos of them caught in the act. Keem would *never* do something like that to me. Then again, that's what Sade thought until her boyfriend did it to her.

When I met Sade one of the first things she asked me was, "You ever been with a white guy? I am *so* over these trifling Negroes."

I started to shake and before I knew what I was doing I'd told her all about Trevor. That's when Sade told me she'd tried to kill herself last summer. The video her sixteen-year-old boyfriend made while they were having sex for the first time went viral. When her parents found out, Sade locked herself in the bathroom and downed a bottle of her mother's anti-anxiety meds. She said she thought that was a better option than having her reputation ripped to shreds when school started up again. But her dad broke down the bathroom door and they took her to the ER to have her stomach pumped.

Sade begged her parents to let her change schools but they refused. So when September rolled around, Sade started eighth grade with a totally different look—thick, blue extension braids hung down her back and swept across her face like a curtain. Every few weeks she'd show up with a new piercing even though her folks kept grounding her to make her stop. Sade wasn't hiding but her new look made her a definite outsider. A freak—like Jamal, Darnell, and me.

Sade's still bitter about what happened—and she has every right to be. Someone she loved and trusted betrayed her. I never felt that way about Trevor but Sade and I bonded just the same. Before long we were best friends, which is why she's the only person I told when I started seeing things.

I thought maybe I was hallucinating, but Sade said her therapist told her that our minds sometimes do funny things after we've had a traumatic experience. Sade said that what happened on base in Germany qualifies as traumatic, so we figured maybe that's why my eyes kept playing tricks on me. Sade offered to get some of her brother's weed for me, but I wasn't sure that would help. I mean, if I saw crazy stuff when I was sober, what would I see once I was high? I kept hoping it would stop just as suddenly as it started, and after my adventure with D and Nuru, for a long while nothing happened. That's when I let myself get closer to Keem.

I haven't told him about the hallucinations, even though I had one while we were out together. Keem was playing ball and I was lined up along the fence with all the gawkers, groupies, and girlfriends. Keem's amazing on court but it was a really hot day and eighty-five degrees is no joke when you're wearing a tight, long-sleeve T under a leather vest and cut-off jeans over fishnet tights—all black, of course. I looked down at my Docs and was tempted to unlace them when I saw this oil stain on the sidewalk. I didn't really stop to think about how it got there—maybe someone chained a motorcycle to the fence post overnight. I just took a moment to admire the pretty rainbow colors on the concrete and then I went back to scanning the court.

It's always easy to spot Keem. He's big—over six feet tall—and broad but lean. When Keem handles a basketball he's *elegant*. I felt proud watching him glide across the court but then the sweat started trickling down my back and so I reached for the water bottle in my bag. And that's when I noticed that the oil spot had moved. It was about a foot away from me before but now the purple outer ring was practically touching the thick rubber sole of my boot. At first I thought maybe I had sunstroke—I was definitely burning up and chugging half a bottle of water didn't help. But when I stepped away from the ring of oil *it followed me*. I took another step back and the oily stain trailed after me over the dry, hot concrete.

I glanced around to see if anyone else noticed what was happening but everyone was absorbed in the game. Suddenly the rainbow ring didn't seem so pretty anymore. It crept toward me like it was getting ready to pounce so I stamped my heavy boot as hard as I could and it *fled*. The stain slid across the concrete and disappeared in the seam of the sidewalk.

I never told Keem about what happened that day at the basketball court. I did tell him about Trevor, though. One day I was feeling kind of low so I went to the library to see if I could find a depressing book to lift my spirits. Nothing makes you feel better about yourself than reading about someone else's crappy life. I was scanning the shelves in the teen room when Keem appeared out of nowhere and wrapped me in this huge bear hug. For some reason I just lost it—I started bawling right there in the library but Keem didn't freak out. He just held me close and let me soak his Knicks jersey with my tears. Afterward we went for a walk along Eastern Parkway. Keem slipped my hand inside his and I avoided his eyes so he wouldn't see the tears filling up in mine. The skin on Keem's palm is calloused from handling the ball so much but he held my hand so gently that day that I finally pulled him over to a bench and told him everything.

"It's not your fault." That's all Keem said when the words stopped tumbling out of my mouth.

"When we first met—in the park that day with D—you said I liked it when guys looked at me." Keem opened his mouth to object but I rushed on. "And you were right—I do want to stand out. I don't want to pretend that I'm normal, because I'm not and I never have been. I mean, my own mother didn't want me! And for a long time I was afraid my dad would leave me too unless I was the perfect little girl. But now it's like—part of me doesn't care anymore. Because everyone leaves eventually."

"Not everyone."

Keem didn't smile. He just looked at me with those dark, solemn, beautiful eyes and for a moment I felt so woozy I had to grip the wooden edge of the bench to make sure I didn't fall off. "I guess I try to stand out because I know that if I blend in with everyone else I'll be invisible. And anything can happen to you when you're invisible."

"Well, I definitely try to stand out on court—I want people to notice me, too." Keem reached over and gently brushed a tear from my cheek. "But that doesn't give anyone the right to hurt you."

That was the first time we kissed. My heart was beating so fast I thought I was going to pass out. *I'm one messed up girl*, I thought to myself as I finally pulled my lips away from Keem's. *But at least now he knows.*

When Keem and I started hanging out more, Cal went berserk. I don't know why—D was with us most of the time, serving as chaperone. Keem and I were together but not *together*, if you know what I mean. We made out once in a while but we weren't glued to each other like some couples I know. Still, Cal felt it was his fatherly duty to get on my case every other day.

"I don't like you spending so much time with this boy."

It was a warm Saturday in June. The school year was almost over so it's not like we had any homework to do. I was sitting on the stairs lacing up my boots. A fight with my father would only spoil the fun day I'd planned with D and Keem so I kept my mouth shut.

"You want to be careful about the company you keep, young lady."

Behind Cal, Sachi was watching me, silently pleading with me to let it slide. I looked at the floor and considered the consequences of my words. Then I lifted my eyes and stared my father in the face.

"What about the company *you* keep, Cal?"

"Excuse me?"

"Sachi's a good person but she isn't perfect, right? She's made some mistakes and you still love her. So why do you expect me to lock myself in my room until the perfect guy knocks on our door?"

Cal couldn't believe I got in his business like that. He ignored what I said about Sachi and focused on my clothes instead. "What kind of guy do you think you'll attract when you dress like that?"

"Like what, Cal?" I was wearing cropped cargo pants, and THREE tank tops under a shredded denim jacket.

"I don't understand why you have to make such a spectacle of yourself. You were such a pretty girl—"

"Yeah—and look where that got me," I muttered under my breath. Sometimes I wonder if Cal thinks I'm "asking for it." In the self-defense class I took they told us clothes have nothing to do with sexual assault, but I wear layers just the same.

Cal tried a softer approach. "I just don't want you to attract the wrong kind of attention."

I finished lacing my boots and stood up. "Guess what, Cal? When I'm out with Keem, no one bothers me. *No one.*" It's true. Guys look at me, then they look at Keem, and they keep on moving. If I were out with my girls, we'd be "fair game" but guys will respect the property of another guy. And that's what I look like when I'm out with Keem—his property.

"Being with an athlete might make you feel important…"

"Being with Keem makes me feel *safe.*"

That shut Cal up for a few seconds. I looked at him and saw what he was thinking: *that used to be my job*.

He cleared his throat and went on. "I know you think I'm out of touch, Nyla, but I was young once. I remember what it's like to be a teenage boy. These ball players—they're used to getting a lot of attention, especially from young women. And all that adoration goes to their head—they don't think the rules apply to them."

Sachi tried to stop things from escalating. "They're going to Coney Island, Cal. What's the big deal? You've met Keem—he's a nice young man."

Cal looked at me. I could tell he was almost ready to let it drop. Then he took a step closer to me and lowered his voice. "You sure you can trust yourself to pick the right one?"

I hated Cal then. Hated him for saying out loud what the voice in my head had been whispering for weeks. But Keem *is* the right one—he definitely belongs on my List of Good Guys and he's *nothing* like that prick Trevor.

My father can be a real jerk sometimes but then it's not like Mr. Diallo's any better. He works two jobs so I've only met him once but it was clear he didn't approve of Keem spending time with me. I wore a boring, ugly outfit that day but it didn't help. I just sat on the plastic-covered sofa in their living room with Gran's aspirin between my knees, knowing that even without my piercings and funky hair I'd never be the kind of girl Mr. Diallo would pick for his son. But that's okay because Keem picked me, and his choice is the one that counts.

If Mr. Diallo had his way, Keem wouldn't even be in Brooklyn right now—he'd be in Senegal taking care of his grandmother instead of spending the summer playing ball and hanging out with me. Keem wants to be a good son and earn his father's respect, but he only met his grandmother once and he was a baby then. She came over to the US to see Keem but not Nasira, even though she was born first. Apparently a granddaughter wasn't worth the trip.

Mrs. Diallo isn't as uptight as her husband but she's still pretty strict. She's always nice to me but I can tell she doesn't understand why Keem would choose a freak like me when he could have his pick of pretty girls. Still, Mrs. Diallo likes that I'm a straight-A student and I'm always super polite when I go over there. Plus Keem wants me around and in that household, what Keem wants Keem gets. His mom isn't about to send him overseas either. Keem's her only son, which means he's her favorite and Mrs. Diallo doesn't bother trying to hide it.

She did stand up for Nasira, though. Back in March one of their neighbors saw Nasira at Fulton Mall and she wasn't wearing her headscarf. Mr. Diallo went berserk and threatened to send Nasira to Senegal immediately, but Mrs. Diallo said her daughter wasn't going anywhere until she graduated from high school and finished at least one year of college. A couple of weeks later Nasira got accepted to Vassar—with a full scholarship. Her dad's proud but he still feels like his kids are slipping away, becoming too American.

"He chose to come here," Mrs. Diallo said once while I was over. "He made this place his home and now he wants to send our children away?"

When I asked her if she ever thought about taking Nasira and Keem back to Bangladesh, Mrs. Diallo shook her head and said, "Never." Then she dished me up a plate of joloff rice and ilish mach.

Mrs. Diallo is an amazing cook but Keem had to beg her to teach him how to prepare food. Why should he learn to cook when his wife will do that for him? Nasira, on the other hand, couldn't care less about making biriyani rice, which makes her mother furious. "How will you ever find a suitable husband?"

Nasira rolled her eyes. "I'm going to college, Ma—and law school after that. If I get married it'll be 'cause I *want* to, not 'cause I *have* to."

"College or no college, if you don't know how to cook no decent Muslim man will have you."

Nasira winked at me. "So maybe I'll marry a man who's not Muslim."

Mrs. Diallo almost choked on her shock. "Not Muslim!"

Nasira messes with her mother the way I mess with Cal. Last month she even made Mrs. Diallo cry by saying she could marry a woman now that gay marriage is legal in New York State. Nasira will have plenty of options if she ever does decide to get hitched. She's a shorter, curvier version of Keem with the same long eyelashes, dark chocolate skin, and thick, curly hair.

That day Keem wrapped his mother up in his long arms and assured her that Nasira was only joking. While he was comforting Mrs. Diallo in the kitchen, Nasira took me to her bedroom to show me all the gear she'd bought for her dorm room. A colorful, striped comforter sat in the corner. Around it were piled matching sheets and towels, a toaster, microwave, plastic cups and plates, and a shower caddy.

"I'm so jealous," I confessed, flopping onto her bed. "I can't wait to move out. My stepmom's cool but Cal is a total pain in the ass."

"Uh—you've met *my* dad, right? Talk about a control freak."

Something glittery hanging in Nasira's closet caught my eye. "What's that?" I asked, pointing to it.

Nasira groaned. "Just this hideous salwar kameez my mom makes me wear for special occasions."

"It's not hideous," I said, moving over to the closet so I could finger the silky green tunic dotted with silver sequins.

"Like you'd ever be caught dead in something like that. The Senegalese dresses my grandmother sends me are even worse. I can't wait to be in a place where I can finally wear whatever I want!"

"Does that include your headscarf?"

Nasira tossed her long, curly hair over her shoulder and shrugged. "Maybe, maybe not." Then the mischief left her eyes. "Did Keem tell you? I picked the dorm where the international students live."

"Why? You were born here—you're American."

"And Muslim. And African. And South Asian. I figured I'd feel more at home with the other foreigners. We can all be outsiders together."

"I hear you," I said. I'd been living in Brooklyn for almost a year and I still felt like a tourist half the time. "What are these?" I asked, pulling out two hangers with neatly folded silken fabric.

"Saris. I'd almost forgotten they were in there." Suddenly Nasira reached over and grabbed my arm. "Here—check this out."

I followed Nasira into her parents' bedroom and watched as she opened a small metal trunk at the foot of the bed. "This is the sari my mom wore on her wedding day."

I gazed at the neatly folded rectangle of deep red silk embroidered with sparkling gold thread. "Wow—that's gorgeous!"

"You should see all the bling Ma wore that day. If I hadn't gotten a scholarship, her gold jewelry could have paid for half my tuition." Nasira unfolded the sari and ran her hand over the gold embroidery along its border. "Of course, her folks didn't come to the wedding so they never saw how beautiful she looked."

"Were they still in Bangladesh?"

Nasira shook her head. "Queens." The she handed me the wedding photo of Mr. and Mrs. Diallo that was on the dresser. "What's wrong with this picture?"

Mrs. Diallo was *drenched* in gold, including a chain that ran from her nose ring to her left ear. Mr. Diallo was a foot taller than his young bride, and looked very dignified in an ivory boubou with gold embroidery around the collar. I looked at their smiling faces and couldn't see anything wrong. "Your folks look really happy. And they're both Muslim, so what's the problem?"

"Dad's African—a *black* African. That didn't go over too well with Ma's family. I met one of my aunts when I was little and a week later she sent me this big jar of skin bleaching cream. I was six!"

I sucked my teeth and handed back the framed photo. "That's messed up. I thought black folks were the only ones using that stuff."

"'Fraid not. Brown folks everywhere have drunk the 'light is right' Kool-Aid. Hey—" That familiar flicker of mischief brightened Nasira's brown eyes. "Want to try it on?"

When Mrs. Diallo came in and saw what we were up to, she didn't pitch a fit like I thought she would. She just told Nasira to go put on her own sari and then she helped me adjust the silk so that it hung in pleats from my waist. I crunched all the gel out of my spiked hair and slicked it back into a ponytail. Mrs. Diallo thought that was a definite improvement but she still draped a sheer red veil over my head, pulling the stiff gold border down until it nearly covered my eyes.

"There. Much better."

Nasira came back into the room looking stunning in her sea green sari. We giggled like little girls and put lipstick and eyeliner on while Mrs. Diallo went through her jewelry box, handing us glittering bangles and jingling anklets to wear. Keem came in after a while and parked himself next to the full-length mirror that hung on the wall. He folded his arms across his chest and watched us with this strange smile on his face.

Nasira took a pillow off the bed and threw it at him. "Quit staring at Nyla, Keem. You're making her blush!"

"A bride should be modest," Mrs. Diallo said in my defense.

I tried to pull the veil down over my eyes to hide my embarrassment but Nasira yanked it back and spun me around to face Keem. "Doesn't she look *exotic*?"

"'Exotic?' Where do you get these ideas?" Mrs. Diallo shooed her daughter away and reached up to straighten my veil. "Nyla looks like a perfectly respectable Bangladeshi girl!"

"She looks beautiful," Keem said quietly, making me blush even more.

Fortunately Nasira grew tired of teasing me. "You got your phone, Keem? Take some pictures and make it quick—this sari's starting to itch."

Keem only managed to take a few shots before Nasira grabbed his phone and made the two of us pose for a picture. Then she flashed the phone at her mother. "Look at the happy couple, Ma."

Mrs. Diallo looked at the image and smiled before handing me the phone. Even though Keem wasn't wearing a boubou, we looked a lot like his parents in their wedding photo.

After we'd changed, Keem called us into the kitchen to devour the feast he'd prepared and the four of us sat around the table and talked for hours. When I look at those photos now I realize how close to perfect that day was. Even after Mrs. Diallo's wedding sari was back in the trunk and I was wearing my "regular" messed up clothes, even though I still looked like the freak that I am, I felt like I belonged.

I keep telling Keem he and his mom should start their own

restaurant, but Keem says his father would never allow it. "Besides," he told me, "my mother thinks her place is here, in the home. She's a traditional Muslim woman. That's why my father married her."

Keem says he likes that I'm feisty and unpredictable, but some days I can't help thinking he'd be better off with some other kind of girl. I told him about Trevor but I haven't told him about everything else—the oil stain, the fire at the library, the eagle in the park. Some secrets are harmless. Others—not so much.

4.

I take my time walking up Vanderbilt. Keem and I agreed to meet in front of the library at two, but I know he'll be a few minutes late. Keem's got basketball camp this summer. It ends at noon but lots of guys hang out in the park, waiting for a chance to play against the best. Folks say Keem will get drafted in a year or two—he's that good. But Keem's got other plans. Last week he asked me which colleges I'm thinking about applying to. When I asked why, he just shrugged. Keem's sweet like that. College is four years away. I guess he thinks we'll still be together then. I'm not such an optimist. A lot can happen in four days, never mind four years.

While Keem's playing ball, D's downtown taking an AP math course at this community college. At the rate he's going, D's going to graduate from college before either of us! D's advanced when it comes to academics but he's still way behind on the social front. I've tried to introduce D to some of my friends but he acts like he doesn't need anybody but me and Keem. That's a dangerous strategy, I tell him. That's how you end up alone.

On Fridays Keem and I pick D up after his class ends at three. We grab some food and hang out in Rockefeller Park for a while. I'll probably be there a lot in the fall. I start at Stuyvesant in three weeks. It's nice over there on the edge of the city. With all those skyscrapers it's easy to forget that Manhattan's an island—Brooklyn too.

Before long I reach Grand Army Plaza, one of my favorite

places to hang out. In some ways, this part of Brooklyn reminds me of Europe. In the middle of the roundabout there's a big triumphal arch to commemorate the Union victory in the Civil War. Like in Europe, the monument isn't off limits—it's a regular part of the landscape and people can stroll around the arch on the sand-colored gravel. A bit farther down there's an ornate fountain with figures from Greek mythology, and around the plaza there are statues of dead white men on horseback. But unlike Europe there are black and brown folks everywhere. They call New York a concrete jungle but Brooklyn is really green. Brooklyn is beautiful.

I'm early and it's hot out so I decide to wait inside with all the other Brooklynites soaking up the library's free air conditioning. The library is built in the shape of an open book. Its spine faces Grand Army Plaza and the tall columns on either side of the entrance are covered with engraved golden images of people and different mythical creatures—a dinosaur, a dragon, a winged horse, and a phoenix. All the people are white, of course, and only the men have clothes—the women are naked.

As I walk up the stairs that lead to the entrance I feel my heart speeding up. Not because of the exercise but because of the memory burned into my brain. Still, I force myself to stop before the image of the golden phoenix. I move in close to avoid all the people going in and out of the library's revolving doors. I look at my fingertips. The skin has healed but I can still feel a strange tingling. Did I dream it? The pain felt real enough at the time. I will my hand to reach out and lightly trace the flames that threaten to engulf the dying bird.

"Careful," warns a male voice from behind. "You don't want to get burned—again."

I spin around and find myself looking at my own startled reflection. A light-skinned black man wearing black cataract glasses is smiling at me. A scruffy grey goatee circles his mouth like a ring of smoke. "It's dangerous to play with fire," he says. "But then you already know that, don't you?"

I feel a string of curse words forming in my mind but panic squeezes my throat shut. What's this guy talking about? He couldn't know what happened before—could he? Without seeing his eyes I can't be sure he's as crazy as he sounds. I move away from the entrance and lean up against the library wall so I can get a better look at him. He's dressed like a normal person: khakis, a black t-shirt, and a white Kangol turned to the back. On his left wrist is a fancy watch—the kind divers wear. He might not be crazy but I decide to ignore him just the same. He seems like he's about Cal's age so why's he trying to talk to me? He could be a perv. There are plenty of them in Brooklyn.

This guy doesn't try to push up on me, though. He puts his hands in his pockets and just stands there in front of the phoenix, forcing people to go around him as they enter the library. The metal bin for returned books fills the space between us. "The phoenix is an ancient symbol of rebirth," he says. "The old bird goes up in flames and a new bird emerges from the ashes."

I'm pretty sure he's looking at me but I can't really tell because of his weird sunglasses. In case he is watching me, I pull out my Swiss army knife, open the blade, and start cleaning under my nails. In my head I develop an action plan. Keem will be here soon, there are security guards just inside the library, and I can see a bored-looking cop strolling along the street below. The library's terrace is full of people—little kids are playing in the embedded fountains on the lower level and all kinds of adults are relaxing at the shaded tables that ring the café cart. But if there's one thing I've learned about New Yorkers, it's that they mind their own business and leave you to handle yours. If this guy starts something, I need to be ready.

"It's time for you to be reborn, Nyla." He says this without looking at me—or that's what I assume since his face is still turned toward the phoenix.

I keep the knife blade open but lower my hand to my thigh. I don't want to talk to him but I can't help myself. "How do you know my name?"

He turns his head slightly so I know that he's looking at me. "I know more than your name. I know you've been struggling with your transition. I know you have questions that I can answer." He pauses and then turns to face the park on the opposite side of Flatbush Avenue. "I know you see what others cannot." The wide black glasses return to my face. "It's a gift, Nyla. There's nothing wrong with you."

I try to hide it but I know he can tell that I'm starting to freak out. Every part of me is trembling, including my voice. "Who are you?"

"My name is Osiris."

I laugh to show my disdain. "You're no god."

A small smile pulls at his lips and he nods with something like humility. "You're right, I'm not. I'm a guide. *Your* guide."

"I look lost to you?"

His smile disappears and his forehead wrinkles with concern. "Yes, you do. But you're not alone, Nyla. There are others like you. I could take you to them."

"And force me to join some kind of cult? No thanks, psycho."

"It's natural for you to be afraid—"

My eyes sweep over the bustling terrace. I see Keem crossing Eastern Parkway and grow bolder, knowing he'll reach me soon. "I'm not scared of you."

"You have no reason to fear me. But you *are* afraid, Nyla—of yourself. Of the person you're destined to become."

I can't find a comeback for that so I keep my lips shut and watch Keem approach. He can tell I'm upset and I know he feels me trembling when he reaches the top of the stairs and takes my arm.

"You alright?" Keem inserts himself between me and Osiris.

They're about the same height but Keem probably isn't even half this guy's age.

Irritation turns down the corners of Osiris' mouth. "You must be Keem," he says flatly.

Keem turns and gets in the guy's face. "Who're you?"

Osiris doesn't back off—he doesn't even flinch. "A friend."

Keem turns back to me for confirmation and somehow having him there as a physical shield restores my confidence. "You're not my friend. I don't even know you." Then I think back to my self-defense class and raise my voice a few notches. "So back off, asshole!"

I grab Keem's hand and pull him after me as I dash down the stairs. All I want is to get on the train and get out of here. If I could I'd sink through the concrete terrace and disappear.

Osiris makes no move to follow us but raises his own voice and calls out, "Avoiding the problem won't make it go away, Nyla."

Keem stops short and turns to confront the man but I tug at him until he follows me over to the street. We have to wait for the light to change before we can cross the stream of traffic swirling around Grand Army Plaza.

"What's he talking about?" Keem asks.

"He knows," I say softly, more to myself than to Keem.

"Knows what?"

I squeeze Keem's hand and glance up at the bare pillar on the other side of the street. Four pillars, three blue eagles with wings raised, poised for flight. "He knows I'm…different."

Keem looks behind us but Osiris hasn't moved from where we left him. "I know that. Everyone knows that."

I shake my head. "He knew about the phoenix. How could he know about that?"

The light changes but I am so lost in my own thoughts that Keem has to pull me across the street. I don't want to go into

Prospect Park so Keem leads us through the huge triumphal arch and into the smaller park in the center of the plaza. We walk in silence, my hand folded inside Keem's, until we reach the Neptune fountain. Keem guides me over to a bench and I sit down next to him, my eyes locked on the square cobblestones radiating outward like waves. Jets of water shoot in graceful arcs over the frozen lovers, and the breeze blows a faint mist onto our skin.

"Nyla?"

I hear Keem calling my name but it is his touch that rescues me from the rising sea of hysteria. Keem turns my face towards his. "Can you tell me what's going on?" he asks gently.

I press my lips together and hope the crust of water-proof mascara on my lashes will keep the tears at bay. I want to lock Keem's fingers between mine but I know the truth may scare him away. I let go of Keem's hand and try to find a way to tell this crazy story. "After what happened in Germany…things changed for me."

"I know. You moved to Brooklyn. You started a new school. A lot of things changed."

I nod and try to force the words to pour out all at once but they seem stuck at the back of my throat. "So much changed so fast…I didn't know what it meant at first. I mean, I didn't know what was making it happen. After that night—I changed, Keem."

"It's ok. Nasira says it takes time to heal from…that kind of thing."

I turn to Keem so that he's looking into my eyes, so he knows I'm for real. "That's not what I'm talking about. Something changed inside my head, Keem. Sometimes…I see things that aren't there."

Keem says nothing for a moment. I look into his eyes and see him searching for words that won't bruise me. "You mean—you hallucinate?"

"I thought that's what it was. I thought I was losing my mind!" I say with a humorless laugh. "Then last spring," I pause and take a deep breath. "The phoenix—the one on the wall by the library's front door…"

"What about it?"

I swallow hard. "It burned me."

"What?"

"I know it sounds crazy, but I touched the gold flames—and they were real. I singed the skin on my fingers."

Keem doesn't take his eyes from mine but I can tell he's searching his mind for some kind of reasonable explanation. But there isn't one. I know because I've searched too.

"Keem—he knew."

"Who knew?"

"That guy at the library. He knew about the phoenix. That it burned me." Keem opens his mouth to speak but I rush on. "And he knew about the eagle."

"What eagle?"

"There are four giant bronze eagles on the pillars at the entrance to Prospect Park."

Keem looks over his shoulder to confirm what I just said. Then he turns back to me. "Ok. But what's that got to do with that crazy guy?"

"He's not crazy, Keem. Or if he is, then I'm crazy too. One day I was standing outside the library and—I saw one of the eagles fly away. It…came to life. Its wings started flapping and it lifted itself off the pillar. Then it turned and looked right at me before it flew off. It's gone, Keem."

"Show me."

Keem tries to stand but I pull him back down. "That's the problem—no one else notices. If you look at the pillars you'll see four bronze eagles. But when I look at them, there are only three. And Osiris knew."

"Cyrus?"

"Osiris—that's the guy's name."

Keem makes a face as if to say I shouldn't worry about someone with such a weird name. I don't know why, but I feel a strange need to defend Osiris—or at least to make him into the kind of freak that Keem can tolerate. A freak like me.

"In ancient Egyptian mythology Osiris was a king who was murdered by his brother. He became a god—the god of death. God of the underworld."

Keem still doesn't look impressed. I want to say, "Osiris said there were other people like me," but I don't. Then my phone goes off and I realize we're running late. "It's D," I say, starting a text to let him know we're on our way.

"Why don't you go home," Keem suggests. "I'll pick up D and we'll come by your place. Your mom won't mind if we order in, right?"

For just a moment I think about going back to the library to see if Osiris is still there. To avoid temptation I grab Keem's hand and pull him off the bench. "Sachi won't mind but Cal will." Keem rolls his eyes. I go up on my tiptoes to give him a quick kiss. "Let's go get D. We can talk about this later."

By the time we get downtown D's polishing off his second slice of pizza. Keem and I grab a burger and fries at a fast food joint while D goes to the corner store. He picks out three pints of ice cream: pistachio for himself, cookies and cream for Keem, and dulce de leche for me. We cross the West Side Highway and head for the park.

The only other Black people in the park are a couple of nannies pushing white babies in deluxe strollers. The dull thud of a basketball hitting the court draws Keem's attention away just for a second, but he doesn't let himself get distracted. Instead he loops one long arm around D's shoulder and smiles at me. I smile back and point to a row of empty benches facing the water. We cross the meadow and settle down to have lunch.

D's got keen emotional radar. He always knows when something's up between me and Keem, so we agreed in advance to play it cool and not tell D about what happened at the library. Still, after we scarf down our burgers and start in on the ice cream, D cautiously asks, "You guys okay?"

Keem gives D a playful shove and then reaches for a napkin to wrap around his pint. The ice cream's melting faster than we can eat it in the hot August sun. "We look okay, don't we?"

"You were late," D says quietly, his eyes on the Jersey shore. "I just thought maybe you had a fight or something."

Keem and I exchange glances. Should we tell him? I decide to keep it light.

"It's my fault. I met this weirdo and he wound me up. It took a while for Keem to calm me down again. You know how I get sometimes."

D sucks the nasty green ice cream off his plastic spoon. "What kind of weirdo?"

Keem looks at me over D's head. *Don't go there*, his eyes say. But D hates it when we treat him like a little kid, and I don't want him to think we're keeping secrets from him.

I look for Lady Liberty holding up her torch in the distance as I think about what to say. "Just this guy—*Osiris*."

D doesn't miss a beat. "God of the afterlife."

I nod. "He said he was a guide—like I'd go anywhere with him."

"How was class?" Keem asks, trying to change the topic.

D shrugs. "I don't know—I couldn't really concentrate."

I don't bother to hide my amazement. "Why not? You love algebra."

D shrugs again and avoids my eyes. "Something doesn't feel right."

I wipe my hand on my jeans and then put my palm on D's forehead the way Sachi does when she thinks I'm sick. D groans and flings my hand away.

"I'm not sick!"

"Then what's wrong?" asks Keem.

"Nothing! Nothing specific, at least. I just have a feeling...something's about to happen."

"Something good, I hope."

D doesn't respond. He doesn't smile and he doesn't nudge me back. Instead he just stares out over the river at the passing boats. I suspect he's thinking about Nuru and the ship that took her back to her realm. The ship that left him behind.

D proves me right a moment later. "I've been thinking about something Nuru said to me once. It was about you guys."

"Oh yeah? I thought she only had eyes for you." I wink at D but he still doesn't smile.

"What'd Nuru say about us, D?" Keem asks.

"She said maybe you two were bound to me—just like she was."

I glance at Keem but it's clear he doesn't know how to respond. "But Nuru was, well, she was inside of you."

D nods and looks at the ground so I won't see the ache in his eyes.

Keem finishes the last of his ice cream and chucks the empty pint into a trash bin that's at least twenty feet away. "What's Mrs. Martin making for dinner?"

"You just ate!" I remind him.

Keem pats his lean stomach. "I'm a growing boy. Is it meatloaf night?"

Finally D cracks a smile. "Meatloaf's on Monday. On Friday she makes chili."

"Is it any good?" asks Keem.

D's too sweet to say anything bad about Mrs. Martin's cooking, but I'm not. "Your foster mother's a nice old woman but you need to introduce her to a bottle of Mrs. Dash."

Keem laughs. “It’s all in the seasoning. Think she’d let me play chef, D?”

“Sure—you can cook and Nyla can distract Mercy. That’ll give Mrs. Martin a chance to put her feet up.”

That settles it. We head back to the train station and join the weary nine-to-fivers heading home from work. The subway platform is stifling—packed with people and so hot you can barely breathe. Fortunately a sleek, silver 2 train pulls into the station and we push our way in. The air conditioning’s on but with so many people crammed together you can hardly tell. Keem and I manage to stay together but D gets pushed to the middle of the car.

I mouth, “You ok?” and D nods back at me but he looks a bit funny. Too much ice cream, I figure.

When the train pulls into the next station, passengers get off and a seat opens up. I look at D, expecting him to sit down, but a pregnant woman boards the train and D leaves the seat for her. As more and more people enter the train, Keem slides his arm around my waist to keep us close together. The doors close and the packed train surges forward. I crane my neck to look for D and see he’s found some breathing room at the far end of the car. I watch as he leans back against the sliding doors that lead into the next car. I stand on my tiptoes to make sure D can see me but his eyes are closed. I turn to Keem.

“D doesn’t look so good.”

Keem rubbernecks until he gets a clear view of D. “He’s probably just tired. And it’s mad hot in here. We’ll be back in Brooklyn soon.”

The train rocks as it races toward the next station. Keem holds onto the rail that runs along the ceiling and I hold onto Keem. My lips brush his neck and I taste the salt on his skin. I like that Keem doesn’t douse himself with body spray like other guys. He cleans up after playing ball but I don’t mind a little sweat—it makes him seem real, like less of a pretty boy. Keem *is* fine. I inhale the scent of his warm skin and then check myself and make a mental note to call my mom once we get above ground. Sachi won't mind if I go over to D's. I think she wants more alone time with Cal and he can't avoid her if it's just the two of them in the house. Plus she likes it when I hang out with Keem *and* D. That makes it innocent somehow.

The train stops one more time before heading into the long tunnel that runs under the river. I rest my head against Keem's shoulder and close my eyes. I see Osiris' face—his black sunglasses hiding his eyes and showing me my own reflection. Does he really know who I am? I open my eyes when the train suddenly grinds to a halt. I search for D and find him still propped against the doors, one hand held against his chest, a strange grimace on his face.

I open my mouth to tell Keem that something's wrong with D but my throat suddenly feels like I've swallowed a fiery thorn. I turn my head aside to cough and once I start coughing, I can't seem to stop. Keem reaches into his duffle bag and hands me a bottle of water. The train lurches forward again and slowly picks up speed. Keem fans his fingers across the small of my back and holds me steady as I open the bottle and gulp down as much water as I can. The scratching in my throat turns into a sharp ache.

Just as I lift the bottle to my lips again the lights on the train go out. Blue sparks spray the blackness outside the train window and we hear the screech of metal on metal as the train follows a turn in the track. As I tip back my head to thirstily suck in another mouthful of water, out of the corner of my eye I see a ghostly face peering at me through the train window. I blink and it's gone. I think I must be having another hallucination but then a moment later, D disappears. The doors behind him open, a gloved hand covers his mouth, and D is pulled out into the blue-black void.

"D!"

I try to scream but my aching throat barely lets out a whisper. I drop the open bottle of water and ignore the complaints of other passengers as I press my way through the twenty bodies separating me from the train doors where D stood just a moment ago. The lights flicker on again just as the doors slide shut with a quiet click. I pull the doors apart again and step into the space between the two train cars. I call D's name as loud as I can but the roar of the train drowns out my weak voice. I try to open the next car's doors but they're locked.

"Where is he?" shouts Keem, stepping into the small space between the two cars.

I grip the chains that link the cars and try to think. *He knew—D* knew *something was going to happen.* We should have listened to him. Before Keem can say anything else I push past him and start moving again. If I can make it to the last car of the train I'll have a view of the tracks. D might be down there—hurt, alone.

"Move—MOVE!" The fire that started in my throat is now spreading to my chest. I fight my way through the passengers who are acting like it doesn't matter that a boy was just snatched off the train. Keem is calling me but I can't stop. People curse at me and shove back as I plow through them to reach the doors that lead to the next car. Just as I reach for the door handles Keem grabs me and pulls me back.

"Nyla—chill!"

I try to shove Keem away from me but he presses me up against the closed doors. With his hands on my shoulders he looks into my eyes and tries to calm me down.

"As soon as the train stops we'll get off and go back for him. But you got to calm down, Nyla. Freaking out doesn't help D."

I nod and try to swallow but my throat is on fire and my lungs feel like they're about to collapse. It seems like forever but less than a minute passes before the train slows as it pulls into the station. We're in Brooklyn now. Keem holds me tight and ushers me off the train.

The crowd on the platform thins as the train pulls out of the station. We're just about to jump down onto the tracks when we hear a voice.

"Have you lost something? Or should I say *someone*?"

I spin around and see Osiris—still wearing his oversized sunglasses even though we're underground. I let loose a string of curses in every language I know and lunge at him but he doesn't move—he doesn't *need* to move because a sudden wave of nausea doubles me over and nearly knocks me onto the tracks.

Keem grabs my arms and pulls me back from the platform edge. I want to push him away but I'm not sure I could stand without his help. I am out of control. I *know* I am out of control but I can't seem to rein myself in. The rage inside me is so strong it feels like I could spew flames. My chest aches, I can barely breathe, and if Keem's arms weren't wrapped around me I'd probably sink onto the filthy platform.

Osiris cocks his head like a bird and watches me. "You're unwell, Nyla. You need help."

My voice is hoarse but still menacing. "What have you done with him? WHAT HAVE YOU DONE?"

"I haven't done anything." Osiris holds out his empty hands as if to prove his innocence. "I'm simply a guide without a follower."

"If you hurt him—" Keem speaks in a low voice that would have shaken any other man.

Osiris just ignores him. He takes a step closer and speaks to me as if I'm a child. "We would never hurt him—or you. Our goal is to help you, Nyla. Your young friend merely serves as an incentive for you to accept our invitation, nothing more."

"Where is he?" Keem asks.

"With the others—in the deep." Osiris casually consults the strange watch on his wrist. "I'd say he's at least three levels down by now."

I take a deep breath and remember Keem's words: *freaking out doesn't help D.* I exhale and try to let go of the anger that's roiling inside of me. After a few seconds I feel my body cooling down and I find the strength to stand on my own. "Bring him back—unharmed—and I'll go with you."

"Nyla, what are you doing?"

I answer Keem but keep my eyes on Osiris. "Negotiating."

Osiris smiles with what seems like genuine pleasure. "Why not come with me now and retrieve your friend? He's had a frightening experience. I'm sure it would be a comfort to him to see you rather than me."

Keem shakes his head, warning me not to accept the offer. But my mind's made up. "Take us to him," I say with resolve.

Osiris nods like a servant. "As you wish. This way, please."

Keem tugs at my hand but doesn't try to hold me back. We follow Osiris to the front end of the platform. Another train pulls into the station and when the doors open, the three of us get on board. Osiris picks up a newspaper left behind by an exiting passenger and ignores us while scanning the headlines.

"You sure about this?" Keem whispers in my ear.

I shake my head but keep my eyes on Osiris. "No. But what choice do we have? D needs us."

When we reach the Grand Army Plaza stop, Osiris guides us off the train and we join the herd of passengers tramping upstairs into the late afternoon heat. The August sun burns overhead in a cloudless blue sky. Traffic whirls around the plaza. On a side street an ice cream truck plays its jingle, luring kids to the curb for a frozen treat. Everything in Brooklyn seems normal—but it's not.

Osiris leads us through traffic to the massive triumphal arch in the center of the plaza. He waits a moment to allow pedestrians to pass by and then heads around the side where the bushes and flowerbeds are. Pulling a key from his pocket, Osiris opens a small, knobless door in the side of the arch and gestures for us to enter. I disentangle my fingers from Keem's and step inside to find myself standing on a small landing in the middle of a wrought iron spiral staircase. I turn back and ask, "Up or down?"

Osiris points at the ground and so I grip the thin railing and cautiously begin to descend the narrow triangular steps. Keem comes after me but we both freeze when Osiris pushes the outer door shut, erasing the light from outside.

"Take these," he says from above. We look back and see that Osiris has donned a yellow hardhat. A small, bright light fixed to the center of his hat allows us to reach for the identical hats he's offering. We take a moment to put them on and then descend the stairs in silence. I can hear water dripping below and occasionally the staircase shakes as a subway train rumbles through a nearby tunnel. When I finally reach the bottom I find myself in some sort of mechanical utility room. Osiris walks off, leaving Keem and I alone in the damp, dark space. I can hear the fast scratching of rats' claws scampering across the concrete floor and we both sigh with relief when Osiris flips a loud switch that brings bright fluorescent light into the room.

"Take these."

Keem and I walk over to the wall where several neon orange safety vests are hanging on hooks. We each pull a vest on and then watch in silence as Osiris yanks back a metal gate to reveal—an elevator.

"You got to be kidding me," I hear Keem mutter under his breath. The elevator looks like it's used to move freight—the floor is blackened with dirt and a wire cage covers a lone light bulb in the elevator's ceiling. It can hold about six people and there are dingy canvas straps screwed into the three walls.

Osiris turns to me. "How do you feel?"

To my surprise, I actually feel much better. It's as if being in this dark, dank space has extinguished the flames that were searing my throat and lungs. "Better," I say quietly, not wanting to give him credit for the improvement. But at this point I have to admit that Osiris seems to know what he's doing. I'm still nervous and it's clear that Keem is too, but this doesn't feel like a dream or a hoax—it feels real. And we never would have found D on our own so I'm glad Osiris offered to show us the way.

Still wearing his dark glasses, Osiris extends his arm to welcome us into the elevator. He pulls the metal gate shut and then says, "Hang on," before pressing a series of buttons on the elevator's front panel. A heavy door slides shut and then the elevator *drops*. Keem and I are thrown back against the walls and I feel my feet lifting off the floor. Osiris nods at the canvas straps and repeats the command we failed to follow: "Hold on!" He has to yell because the elevator is as loud as a train hurtling through a tunnel.

Keem and I seize the straps with both hands and hold on as if our lives depend on it. I feel the food I ate before churning in my stomach and try my best not to heave it up. I can't help feeling that all of this is a test. I don't know what it's supposed to prove, but I definitely don't want to screw up.

Finally, after an agonizing minute that felt more like an hour, the elevator begins to slow down and then comes to a fairly gentle stop. The carriage bounces a couple of times and then Osiris presses a large green button and the inner door slides open. To my surprise, a young white woman wearing a hardhat and orange vest pulls open the outer metal gate.

"Going up?" Osiris asks pleasantly.

She just glares at him, impatiently waits for us to exit, and then takes our place inside the elevator without saying a word.

"Don't mind Roan," Osiris says with a tight smile. "She's always cranky at the end of a long shift."

"What do you do down here?" Keem asks.

"You're miners," I say, somewhat disappointed.

Osiris looks around at the tunnel before dismissing my guess. "Not exactly. Everything will become clear in time. Now, if you'll just follow me, I'll take you to your friend."

5.

I am not alone. Nuru is with me!

Even before I'm snatched off the train, I know something is happening to me. All day I've felt weird—like something is moving inside of me, fighting for space. Then the man grabs me from behind and I feel a kind of explosion in my chest. I know right away that it's Nuru because I'm not as scared as I ought to be—my heart feels light and I'm able to stay calm because I know that Nuru won't let anything terrible happen to me. The white man binds my hands with a plastic loop—the kind cops use instead of handcuffs. He says he won't tape my mouth shut if I promise not to cry for help. Then he puts a sack over my head and tosses me over his shoulder.

I can't tell where we're going but we stay in the subway tunnel for quite a while—I know because I hear trains passing every few minutes. Then we start going down different sets of stairs until we reach some sort of elevator. I nearly lose my lunch when it drops so fast. But Nuru's with me so I try not to panic. When the man finally sets me down and pulls off the sack, I see that my right hand is glowing. I quickly pull my sleeve over my hand and look around. I'm in some kind of cave. The rock is black and wet and the air around me feels cool. I shiver and ask, "Where am I?"

"No questions—just sit tight. We'll let you go once we get what we want. Make a fuss or try to escape and we'll leave you down here—forever." A nasty smirk twists the scar on his face and he walks away whistling in the dark. I wait a moment and then try to follow the sound as best I can. Groping my way in the dark, I discover that I'm in a tunnel that leads to a much larger cavern. A big industrial lamp is set up on the far side of the cavern and near it I can see a woman wearing a hardhat. She looks like some kind of surveyor with her fluorescent vest and measuring rod. What would a bunch of miners want with me?

"You're late, Liev," she says, making me wonder if she's his boss.

The sound of the woman's voice somehow gives me hope. I creep along the wet wall of the tunnel until I can see them both.

"Sorry," says the man who kidnapped me. "Had a job to do." He points upward and that seems to pique the woman's interest.

"Oh yeah?"

"Yeah." Liev goes over to the base of the metal lamp and picks up a yellow hardhat. He turns on the attached light before placing the hat on his bald head. "Siris asked me to snatch some kid off the train."

The woman frowns. "A kid? What's he want with a kid?"

Liev shrugs and says, "Bait, I guess."

The woman mutters something but I can only make out a couple of curse words. "Where is this 'bait'?" she asks.

"Over there," Liev says, flinging a careless hand in my direction.

"You left the poor kid alone in the deep?" she asks angrily.

Liev scowls at her. "Siris told me to snatch him and bring him here. He didn't say anything about babysitting the brat."

"You're heartless, Liev."

He shrugs again. "You want to go hold his hand? I left him back there in the east tunnel."

I press myself against the tunnel wall and listen to the heavy footsteps heading toward me. There isn't time to go back to the place Liev left me so I just hide Nuru's light and hope for the best. In a moment the pretty brown-skinned woman comes around the corner. She's wearing work boots, cargo pants, and a black t-shirt under her bright orange vest. Her face and bare arms are smeared with dirt. She looks tired but not unkind.

"Hey there," she says with a smile. "I'm Lada."

I flinch as the bright light on her hardhat shines in my eyes. She apologizes and pulls the hat off. Then she notices my bound hands and says, "Here—let me get that for you." Before I can say anything she sets the hat on the ground, whips a box cutter out of her pants pocket, and cuts through the tight plastic loop. "That's better. You okay?" Her hand rests on my shoulder for a moment and I quickly tug my sleeve down. "Welcome to the deep."

I try to peer around her and into the wide cavern. Liev said he'd left me in the east tunnel so there must be a west tunnel somewhere. Is there more than one elevator? I can't see anything that looks like a way out.

Lada pulls the neon green kerchief off her head and smoothes down the spiral curls that have escaped her two braids. "It's alright. No one's going to hurt you—I promise."

"Then why am I here?" I ask.

She sighs and squats down to get a better look at my face. "Probably because someone you know refused our...invitation. We're not the kind of people who take 'no' for an answer."

"Like the mafia?"

She laughs. "No, we're not like the mafia."

"So what kind of people are you, then? I don't have any money—and neither does my foster mother."

Pity softens her voice. "We don't want any money, sweetheart."

"Then why'd you kidnap me?"

Lada sighs and wipes her brow with the back of her hand. "We aren't looking for a ransom. We're looking for...help. It may not look like it, but we're the good guys. Sort of like superheroes—but without the cool costumes."

She smiles at me and for just a moment her face looks familiar to me. I think about what Liev called me—*bait.* "You're after Nyla, aren't you?"

Even in the dim light I can see her face change. The fatigue I saw before disappears and suddenly Lada looks dangerous. She pushes herself up off her haunches and peers more closely at me. "Nyla?"

"She'll come for me—Keem, too."

Something like relief softens the deep lines creasing her brow. "Who's Keem?"

"My other friend. He's big—and really strong. He's an athlete."

Lada nods and tries not to laugh at me. "That's probably who they're after. We could use a big, strong guy right about now."

"Nyla's strong, too," I add, "just in a different way."

"Oh yeah?"

"Yeah. She looks out for me. Keem and Nyla—they'll come for me. I know they will."

"That's what we're counting on," Lada says with a weary sigh. She watches me for a moment longer and then forces herself to smile. "You never told me your name."

"D."

"Well, D, you're lucky to have two loyal friends. Sometimes when we take bait the person we're really after just walks away."

I look down at the threads of light trailing from my sleeve. "Keem and Nyla aren't like that. We've been through a lot together."

She nods and then reaches for my right hand. "May I?"

My eyes dart around the dark tunnel. There's nowhere to run but if I say no, I don't think she'll hurt me. So I nod and barely feel the pressure of Lada's fingers as she takes my hand and pushes back my sleeve. If she expected to find me holding a glow stick or a compact flashlight she shows no sign of surprise. My palm pulses with Nuru's cool, white light but Lada just watches it calmly without saying a word.

"Interesting," she says before letting go of my hand. "I'd keep that under wraps if I were you. Otherwise my colleagues may realize just what a special sort of boy you are."

"You won't tell?"

Lada shakes her head. "We all have secrets here in the deep."

Suddenly a man's voice echoes down a tunnel on the far side of the cavern. "Where's the boy?"

Then Nyla's voice booms in the darkness. "D? Where are you?"

Lada freezes. Then Nyla comes into view and Lada gasps. Then she *explodes*. "SIRIS!"

Lada snatches her hard hat up off the ground and hisses, "I'll kill him!" before storming over to the mouth of the west tunnel, forgetting all about me.

A man wearing black cataract glasses tries to greet her but Lada blows past him and heads straight for Nyla. I watch as Lada shines the light from her hardhat into Nyla's stunned face. Then she backs away saying, "No. Hell no!" over and over again.

I step out of the east tunnel and hurry over to Nyla and Keem who are both wearing hardhats and safety vests. I see them but they don't see me because Lada's about to lose it. She flings her hard hat aside and lunges at the man in the dark glasses. "You bastard!"

Despite being several inches shorter than the man, for a moment it looks like Lada might actually strangle him. Then Liev rushes over and manages to pull her off.

The man in the glasses tries to laugh off the attack. He coughs a bit and then says, "She has quite a temper, don't you think, Nyla?"

Lada struggles with Liev and finally manages to fling him off. "Get off me!" she yells angrily and all of us back away from her. Lada points a shaking finger at the man in glasses. "You have no right bringing her here."

He holds his throat and tries not to sound as shaken up as he looks. "I do my duty, Lada, just as you do yours."

"She's *fourteen*!"

"My orders were to retrieve her. Marta's motives mean nothing to me."

"Liar! You know damn well what's going on here."

He shrugs helplessly but it's clear he's enjoying this exchange. "I don't call the shots, Lada. If you have a problem, take it up with Marta, not me."

"Oh, I will, Siris! You better believe I will."

Lada suddenly grabs Nyla by the arm. "Come on."

Nyla spins and wrenches her arm free. "Who the hell are you?"

Lada holds up her hands. "Take it easy, kid. Let's just get out of here. D—follow me."

"Where are you taking us?" I ask.

"Back home—where you belong."

"Sounds good to me," says Keem. He takes Nyla by the hand but doesn't try to pull her along. Keem waits to see what she wants to do. Nyla glares at the two men in the cave and then puts her arm around my shoulders and we head into the west tunnel.

Lada stomps ahead of us and doesn't say a word as we wait for the elevator to arrive. She just stands there, fists clenched, her eyes drilling a hole into the rocky wall. Then a bell rings, Lada pulls back the metal gate, and waves us inside. She casts a vicious glance over her shoulder but no one back there is foolish enough to try to stop Lada. She gets in, slams the outer gate shut, and pushes a series of buttons that send us shooting upward like a rocket. The ride up is made even more uncomfortable by the awkward silence between us. When the elevator finally comes to a stop, Lada pulls the gate open but stays inside as we file past her into what looks like some kind of storeroom.

"I'm sorry this happened to you," she says without looking at any of us. "I'll do what I can to make sure it doesn't happen again."

Lada reaches for the outer gate but Nyla steps forward and grabs hold of it.

"Who are you?" asks Nyla, trying to peer into the woman's face.

Lada keeps her eyes lowered and without answering Nyla's question gently peels her fingers off the gate. "I'm sorry," she whispers before yanking the gate shut. Then the elevator door closes and Lada drops back into the deep.

"What the hell was that?" Nyla looks from me to Keem as if she really expects us to have the answer.

Keem says nothing and instead takes off his hardhat and orange vest. Nyla follows his lead and they both hang their vests on the hooks that line the wall.

"How did you guys find this place?" I ask.

Now it's Nyla's turn to say nothing. Keem points me in the direction of a spiral staircase on the other side of the room. "We had a guide," he says. "Osiris—the guy who got jumped by that crazy lady."

"I don't think Lada's crazy," I say, grabbing hold of the rusty iron railing. "She was nice to me."

"Oh yeah?"

I stop climbing the stairs and turn to look at Nyla. She's still standing by the elevator. Keem is standing at the foot of the staircase. "Let's go upstairs," he says. "I think we could all use some fresh air."

That sounds like a good idea to me but Nyla doesn't move. "Tell me about her, D."

I glance at Keem and wonder if I should make Nyla wait till we're above ground again. I can tell Keem's worried she's going to get back on that elevator. I can't think of a way to stall so I say, "Lada told me they're the good guys and that they weren't going to hurt me. They just used me as bait."

"Bait?"

"To get to you," I say, looking at Keem. Then I turn to Nyla.

"Or you. That woman—when I said your name…"

Nyla finally moves away from the elevator and draws closer to the staircase. "What happened, D?"

"I don't know," I say, climbing up a few more steps. "Lada sort of froze—like she knew you or something."

Keem gently pushes Nyla up to the stairs, hoping she'll take the hint and follow me. "Have you ever seen that woman before?" he asks her.

Nyla shakes her head and sets her foot on the first step. "No—never."

"Well, I think she knows you," I say, continuing to climb. "She definitely didn't want you down there."

"Osiris did," says Keem, putting his own giant foot on the first step. Nyla's forced to start climbing and soon we're all winding our way up the spiral staircase. "Osiris is the one who planned all of this. He knew he could get to you by messing with D."

"I think he was trying to get to *her*," I say. "It's like he wanted to set Lada off."

"Why would he want to get jumped like that?" asks Nyla.

"Maybe to make her look bad," Keem suggests. "She was definitely out of control!"

I reach a small landing and wait for Nyla and Keem to catch up. The staircase keeps going but Nyla tells me to open the door instead. I turn the knob and pull but nothing happens. Nyla gives it a try, too, but it takes Keem to finally force the door open. We shield our eyes from the bright sunlight and step out into Grand Army Plaza. Nuru taught me that there was a whole other world beneath the city, but I never imagined there could be a world beneath that world.

"You guys still want to come to my place?" I ask.

Nyla shakes her head. "I think I better go home. I'm exhausted."

Keem offers to walk Nyla home and I tag along because, well, that's what I do. We head toward Vanderbilt Avenue.

For a while none of us says a word even though we're all trying to make sense of what just happened. I decide to break the silence. "So…do you think these people are really after you, Nyla?"

She looks like she's far away—still underground or lost somewhere in the past. "Why would a bunch of grimy miners want me?" she whispers.

Nyla really does look tired. Keem has his arm around her and he's got that protective look that makes me think twice about saying anything more. But if we don't figure this out, Nyla won't be safe at all. Who's to say they won't try to snatch *her* next time? I push the words out before they slip back down my throat. "I don't think they're miners."

"Who else hangs out that far underground?" asks Keem.

"Did you see something, D?"

I look at Nyla and know she'd do anything she could to help me. I owe her the truth. "That woman—Lada. She saw my hand. She saw Nuru's light."

Nyla stops walking, forcing me and Keem to stop, too. "And?"

"Well, she didn't act like it was strange. She just told me I was special."

"That just proves she's crazy," says Keem, "which we knew the minute she attacked Osiris."

"Or…" I start. Keem's glare dares me to go on.

"Or—what?" asks Nyla.

I look down at my palm. Nuru's light has disappeared but I know she's still inside of me. "Maybe Lada didn't freak out because she's seen something like it before."

Nyla's eyes open wide. "*Another* Nuru?"

"Maybe. Or something like Nuru. Something…not human."

"Come on. Let's get you home."

Nyla leans into Keem and lets him lead her forward.

I tag along but soon fall behind. It's hard for three people to fit on a Brooklyn sidewalk. I have more things that I want to say but I don't know if Nyla's ready to hear it right now. I know Keem's not. I clear my throat and start talking. I figure they can listen if they want or just ignore me. "When Nuru first came to me, I thought that made me special." Keem glances back at me but Nyla keeps her head buried in his chest.

"I even thought…that maybe my dad had sent Nuru to me so I wouldn't be alone after Mom died."

Nyla stops walking. She gently pushes Keem away and turns to face me. "Just say what you have to say, D."

I take a deep breath, knowing Nyla may bite my head off once these words leave my mouth. "Would you recognize your mom if you saw her today?"

Nyla frowns. Keem thinks she's confused so he says, "D means your birth mother, not Sachi."

Nyla snaps at him, suddenly upset. "I know what he means, Keem!" She tries to check her temper before turning to me. "Listen, D. My biological mother left when I was a little kid. That makes her a heartless bitch, not some sort of freak who lives underground!"

"I'm just saying…"

"I know what you're saying! And you're wrong."

"But how do you know?" I ask quietly. "I mean, you can't be sure she wasn't—"

"Leave it, D!"

Keem doesn't raise his voice very often—and he *is* twice my size—so I keep the rest of my thoughts to myself.

Nyla reaches up and clenches her mane of streaked, spiked hair with both hands. "I'm sorry, you guys. I just—" Nyla's voice breaks and she flicks away two rogue tears that have spilled onto her cheeks. "I just need to be alone for a while," she says wearily. "I'll call you tomorrow, okay?" Then Nyla turns away from us and runs the rest of the way down the block.

"Nice going, D."

Keem wants me to feel guilty but I don't. He stares down the block long after Nyla has disappeared inside her brownstone. "She doesn't need this right now," he says finally.

"I don't know," I say quietly. "Maybe she does."

6.

I turn my key in the lock but take a moment to pull myself together before opening the door. I don't know if I've ever felt this tired before. But as much as I'd love to go upstairs and collapse on my bed, I know the thoughts racing through my head wouldn't let me fall asleep. I need proof and I won't rest until I've got it.

"Hey, Sachi." I drag myself into the kitchen and press my forehead into the cool stainless steel surface of the fridge.

"There you are. I was starting to worry. Everything okay?"

I flop into a chair and tip my head back as far as it will go. "I'm beat. We went all over the city today."

"Are you hungry? I was thinking about ordering in. Feel like Thai tonight?"

I bring my head back up and force myself to smile at Sachi. Food is the last thing on my mind right now but I can't afford to set off any alarm bells. "Mmm—sounds good. I think I'll go clean up a bit. Hey—"

Sachi looks up from the takeout menu in her hands.

"Gran's photo albums—do you remember where we put them?"

"I think they're still boxed up. Check the closet in the spare room."

"Ok, I will—*after* I take a shower," I say, wiping at the grime on my bare arms.

"Do you want spring rolls or dumplings?"

"Spring rolls, please." I wait until Sachi picks up the phone to place our order. Then I head upstairs, forcing myself not to take the steps two at a time. I have to act normal. I go into the bathroom, turn on the shower, and open the window to let out the steam. Then I dash into the spare room, grab the box in the closet, and lock myself in the bathroom.

I don't need to do this because deep in my gut—I *know*. Cal erased all traces of my mother as soon as she walked out on us, and I can't say that I blame him. But once, when I was about ten, I remember asking Gran for a photograph of my mother. And she opened up this tacky old vinyl album that was the color of lima beans. The same album I'm holding in my hands right now.

The first few pages are filled with wedding photographs. Then come the baby pictures and finally I find what I'm looking for. I peel back the clear cover sheet from the stiff, sticky page and remove one of the photos. On the back, in Gran's spidery handwriting, are three words: *Emma and Nyla*. The picture is dated 1990. But it's her—I'm sure of it. Just a few months before she left without saying goodbye, giving a reason, or offering an apology.

I shove the photograph in my back pocket and put the album back inside the cardboard box. Then I turn off the shower and take a good look at myself in the mirror. I splash some water on my face and wet my hair a bit. I roll on a little more deodorant and then head back downstairs.

"You didn't change?"

"Uh—I figured I'd put my pajamas on when I get back. I'm just going to the store. I feel like having cream soda with my green curry." Sachi wrinkles her nose in disgust and reaches for her purse. "Grab some soy milk while you're there—we're almost out."

"Sure." I plant a quick kiss on Sachi's cheek, take the twenty-dollar bill from her hand, and head for the front door. "Where's Cal?" I ask loudly enough so that Sachi can hear me in the kitchen.

She follows me into the hallway and says simply, "Out."

I see the loneliness in my stepmother's eyes and for the first time I wonder if my father might be having an affair. Prick.

Then Sachi says, "Cal's really serious about starting this charter school, you know. He and Don went out to East New York to check out a possible site. He said he might be home late."

I feel like crap now so I smile extra hard. "Girls night, then."

"Yep—girls night. The food should be here by the time you get back."

I grab my keys, open the front door, and stand at the top of the stoop. The sun is setting and the sky over our block of brownstones has a rosy glow. I descend the steps slowly, trying to develop a plan. Should I go over to the library and see if Osiris is there? Or should I wait for him to find me again? I decide to head to the grocery store first. I'll do what I said I was going to do, and if nothing happens tonight I'll go back to Grand Army Plaza first thing tomorrow.

Cal says this neighborhood has changed a lot since my grandparents bought their brownstone in the 1960s. The grocery store never used to sell soy milk and organic fruits and vegetables, but gentrification has changed all that. A tall black man in cataract glasses would definitely stand out now that most of the people who live around here are white. Cal fits in because he's a squeaky clean black man with glasses and a pretty Asian wife.

I stand out, of course, and I'm used to people staring at me but tonight I feel more self-conscious than ever. I'm trying to act cool but every sound seems amplified—the squeaky wheel of an old lady's grocery cart, the trendy ringtone of some hipster's phone. I keep thinking—hoping—that Osiris is going to appear out of nowhere but he doesn't. I pay for the milk and soda and leave the store feeling angry and disappointed at the same time.

The sky is a beautiful shade of purple. I scan Vanderbilt one last time before heading up our block. Sachi doesn't need a self-absorbed teenager to go with her absentee husband. I cross the street and vow to make my stepmother happy tonight. My birth mother abandoned me ten years ago. Wanting to be with her now is just wrong on so many levels.

Just as I reach our stoop a man steps out from between two parked cars. I spin around and instinctively reach in my pocket for my knife. The streetlights have come on but Osiris lingers in the shadows cast by a nearby oak tree.

"What did you think of Lada?" he asks casually. "She makes quite a memorable first impression."

Ten minutes ago I would have been thrilled to see him but right now all I want is for Osiris to get away from my house. "You shouldn't be here," I say angrily. "My stepmom's inside and if my dad sees you—"

"We'll tell him I'm D's uncle," Osiris says with a smile. "You know who Lada is, don't you?"

I know I should walk away but something deep within me is drawn to the confidence in his voice. All I want is the truth. I step into the shadows and face Osiris head on. Somehow his oversized black glasses still show me my reflection. I'm trembling like a bird.

Osiris' lips twist with satisfaction. He's finally caught me and he knows it. "I'm surprised I didn't notice it before—the resemblance is really quite remarkable."

"Why are you doing this?"

"I'm your guide."

"You don't act like it. You act like you're playing some sort of game. This is my life, you know—it's my family you're messing with."

Osiris bows his head slightly, which I take to be his attempt at an apology. In a serious voice he says, "This isn't a game, Nyla. My job is to start you on your journey and there have been too many delays already. We don't have much time." He pauses and actually manages to look humble. "Will you come with me now?"

I look down at the grocery bag and try to come up with a plausible lie for Sachi. "Wait here," I tell Osiris. Then I step out of the shadows and head home.

"Mom?"

"We're in here, Nyla."

Shit. Cal's home. I walk down the hallway and arrange my face for the lie about to spill out of my mouth. Sachi and Cal are standing at the counter unpacking takeout containers filled with Thai food. My stomach grumbles and I wonder if I have time to scarf down a spring roll before going back to Osiris.

"Hey, Daddy." I playfully bump Cal on my way to the fridge. He pokes his elbow in my back and winks at me. That means he's in a good mood. While putting the soda and soy milk away, I give him a chance to talk about his day. "How was the site in East New York?"

"It has potential but it needs a lot of work. And it's pretty far from the train, which is less than ideal."

"Most kids walk to school, don't they?" asks Sachi.

"It's not the students I'm thinking about—it's the staff. We have to attract the very best teachers if this boys academy is going to succeed."

Sachi takes three plates down from the cupboard and passes one to me. This is my cue.

"Um—would it be ok if I go over to Sade's tonight?"

"After dinner? I don't see why not. As long as you don't stay out too late."

"Actually—" I put on a sheepish grin and Cal stops dishing noodles onto his plate. "I'm going to eat over there. Sade just broke up with her boyfriend and I don't think she should be alone right now." I shoot Sachi a meaningful look.

"Sade—isn't she the one who...took those pills before?"

I nod quickly and add, "Her folks are home. I just thought I'd go over and try to cheer her up. She's been texting me all day. You don't mind, do you, Daddy?" I know he likes it when I call him that. It reminds him of the good old days when I was his innocent, little girl. I give my father another playful nudge.

He sighs and says, "So long as you respect your curfew."

"Don't I always?" I grab a spring roll off Cal's plate and shove it in my mouth before ducking out of the kitchen.

Outside I use the back of my hand to wipe the grease off my mouth. I stand in the circle of light cast by the streetlamp and say, "Let's go."

Osiris emerges from the shadows and points down the block. "This way."

We walk in silence for several blocks, leaving the brownstones behind. The rail yard isn't far from here and I wonder if we'll be taking another train. Finally Osiris turns to me and says, "You do know who Lada is?"

I tug the photograph out of my back pocket and flash it at him. "She's my mother—my *biological* mother. I don't need you to tell me that." I swallow hard and try to keep the desperation out of my voice. "Can you take me to her?"

Osiris casts a wary glance down the deserted street. "If you like, though my orders are to bring you to Marta."

"Who's Marta?"

"My boss. *Our* boss. Marta's the one who told me how to find you. She knew it was time."

Time for what? None of this makes sense but there's one person who can explain everything. "I want to see Lada first. I don't really care where we go after that."

Osiris nods in a way that's designed to make me feel like I'm calling the shots. "This way," he says, extending his arm so that I'm allowed to take the lead.

I barely make it around the corner before I hear a groan and then a long, soft sigh. I look back over my shoulder and see Osiris sinking into a mound of black trash bags piled by the curb. Lada stands over him, her face grim.

"What did you do to him?" I ask, more out of curiosity than concern.

"He'll be fine," Lada says flatly. I must not look convinced because she shrugs and adds, "It's like being tasered. The effects are temporary."

I look for a stun gun but her hands are empty.

"What did he tell you?" Lada asks, placing her hands on her hips.

"Nothing I didn't already know. He said he'd take me to you."

She spreads her arms out in a dramatic gesture. "Well, here I am."

There's something both sarcastic and defiant in Lada's pose. I force the words out before rage closes my throat again. "You're my mother?"

"Yes."

She says it simply, without shame and for a while we just stand there staring at one another. Then a low moan comes from the pile of trash and Lada pushes me farther down the block.

"Listen to me, Nyla. You have to stay away from Siris."

"Why? He said he's my guide. He wants me to meet Marta."

"*I* will deal with Marta," she says with a scowl. "*You* need to get out the city—now."

For the second time today she grabs my arm like I'm some kind of doll she can just drag around. I yank my arm free and stop trying to keep my anger in check. "I can't believe this! I waited *ten years* to meet you and you can't wait to get rid of me—again."

Lada looks genuinely surprised. "No! It's not like that."

"Really? That's how it looks to me."

Lada steps back and sighs. "Seeing you...is like a dream, Nyla."

I roll my eyes and she rushes on. "All these years I've wanted to—I mean, I hoped one day I could..." She stops and presses her lips together. I watch as all the tenderness disappears from her face. "You don't know these people like I do," Lada says in a cold, hard voice. "They're lying to you. You saw how they snatched D. They'll do anything to get their hands on you."

I fold my arms across my chest. "Well, at least someone wants me."

Lada frowns. "They only want to *use* you, Nyla. That's what they do. They use people up and then throw them away. Please," she touches my arm gently this time. "Please, just trust me on this. You have to go."

"Why do they want me?"

A huge black SUV cruises past us, its bass throbbing. Lada watches it instead of me. "That's not important—"

"It's important to me," I say. "You want me to trust you? Then tell me the truth. Why do they want me?"

Lada sighs and leans against the metal gate of a closed auto shop. "Because you're my kid."

"That didn't make *you* want me." She winces and I feel a brief surge of satisfaction.

"They're hoping you'll turn out like me."

"What—and be a shitty mother?"

Lada doesn't react this time. "I work underground, Nyla. Deep underground. There aren't many people in the world who can do what I do."

"What is it you *do* exactly?" I try to make her look at me but everything on this block seems more interesting to her.

"There are...*things*...in the deep. I try to keep them from reaching the surface."

"What kind of things?"

Lada sighs impatiently. "Bad things, alright? Evil things."

I stare at my mother without blinking as an image forms in my mind. "You mean you're—like, a slayer?"

Lada rolls her eyes. "This isn't some kind of comic book story, Nyla! I'm not a vampire slayer and I'm not a mutant—and neither are you."

"What are you, then?" Lada takes a few steps away from me so I direct my next question at her back. "And what am I?"

She stops and turns to face me. "Marked. You and I are marked—some say destined—to do this work."

I'm confused—*of course*, I'm confused—but that only seems to irritate Lada. Her lips twist as though something bitter has seeped into her mouth. "The stakes are high, Nyla. This isn't a job. You don't get a salary or a pension."

"There must be some benefits, right? Otherwise, why bother?"

For once I've said the right thing. Lada's face softens. "Benefits? We're beating back the devil, sweetheart. When we succeed, the entire human race benefits."

"And when you fail?"

"People suffer—and die." She turns and walks off, arrogantly assuming I'll scamper after her. And I do.

"Death is part of life. We accept that. And there's evil in the world already—there's nothing we can do about that. But when there's a surge—when a purer source of evil tries to force its way into the world…we stop it. At least we try."

"How?"

Lada reaches up and grabs her hair—just like I do when I'm aggravated. "I can't have this conversation right now, Nyla. All you need to know is that it's not safe for you to be here. Come on—I'll walk you home."

"You know where I live?"

"Of course. I've always known where you were. I couldn't get too close but…I'd stop by and watch you from a distance sometimes." She pauses and shakes her head with regret. "That's probably how they found you. One of them must have followed me."

"If you don't trust these people why do you work for them?"

"It wasn't exactly a choice. I was recruited."

"And now they're trying to recruit me."

Lada gives me a grim nod, then puts a hand lightly on my back and steers me up the block. "Let's get you home."

We walk in silence for most of the way. There are a lot of things I want to say to her—my head's full of accusations—but if this is the last time I'm going to see my biological mother I don't want to come off as a total bitch. When we reach my block I decide I'd better say what I have to say.

"What kind of mother just walks out on her kid?"

Lada stops and takes a deep breath. She had to be expecting this but I can tell she's struggling to find the right words. Finally she sighs and says, "I left because I knew you could manage without me. You had Cal and he had his mother." Lada screws up her lips to say something more but decides not to speak ill of the dead. "Besides, it's not like you were a baby or anything. I waited until you were grown." She starts walking again, hoping to leave the subject behind.

"Grown?" I nearly choke on the word. "I was *four.*"

Lada talks over her shoulder, forcing me to keep up. "You've always been mature for your age. I knew you could handle yourself. You could walk, talk, flush—you didn't need me anymore." She slows her pace and waits until we're walking side by side once more. "Plus…you didn't show any signs. You were clean then. I couldn't risk you picking anything up from prolonged exposure to me."

"It's contagious?"

Lada shakes her head. "Genetic, apparently. But I didn't know then what I know now. I was trying to do the right thing, Nyla. And I'm trying to do that now. So listen to me, ok? Just…lay low for a while. And whatever you do—stay above ground."

"Are you serious? This is New York. How am I supposed to get around if I can't take the train?"

"Get a bike. Take the bus. You're a clever girl—I'm sure you can figure it out." Lada speeds up and heads straight for our stoop. "I need to speak to your father. Now's a good time for a little family vacation."

I practically have to jog to catch up with her. "Are you planning to join us?"

That stops Lada in her tracks. She spins around and finally looks me in the eye. "You really don't get it, do you? I'm *trying* to keep you safe—and that means staying as far away from me as possible."

"Why?"

Lada sighs impatiently and tries not to lose her cool. "I'm trying to buy you some time, Nyla. All I ever wanted was for you to have a normal life. Isn't that what you want—to hang out with your friends like a regular teenager?"

"But you just said I'm not regular. I'm like you."

Without saying another word, Lada takes the stoop stairs two at a time and rings the doorbell.

By the time I reach the top of the stoop with my key, Sachi's already opening the front door. "Yes, may I help you? Nyla! I thought you went—"

"She's with me," I say, pushing past Lada and leading the way inside. "She'll explain everything."

Before Lada can ask for Cal I holler, "DADDY!" with enough neediness in my voice to ensure that my father will respond right away. Then I turn to Sachi. I make a show of kissing her on the cheek and say, "Hey, Mom. This is Lada. She and Cal are old friends." Then I plant myself at the bottom of the stairs and wait to see the look on my father's face.

Cal doesn't disappoint. He takes one look at Lada and freezes halfway down the stairs. Then he grabs the banister, steadies himself, and says, "What are you doing here?"

I open my mouth to respond but Lada's faster than me this time. "I came to warn you, Cal. You need to get Nyla out of the city—*now*."

Cal calmly descends the stairs without saying a word but Sachi panics. "Nyla? Why—has something happened?"

"I'll handle this," Cal says, stepping over me and slipping an arm around her. "Sachi, this is Emma. My ex-wife."

"Actually, it's Lada, and I'm sorry we have to meet this way but I need you to listen carefully to me. If you don't take Nyla out of the city, the people who claimed me ten years ago will claim her, too."

Cal surprises us all by chuckling. "You've got a lot of nerve showing up here like this."

Lada keeps a straight face to prove she's serious. "That's right—I do. But no matter what you think about me, Cal, our daughter's life is at stake here. Take her away—or they will."

"They—they who?" Sachi flings Cal's arm off her shoulder. "What's going on here?"

"Why don't we go into the parlor. Nyla, go to your room."

"Pssshhh. I don't think so," I say with as much respect and resolve as I can manage.

Cal turns on his drill sergeant voice. "*Now*, young lady."

"Leave her alone, Cal. She needs to hear this, too."

Cal spins from me to Lada. "You think you can just walk in here and tell me how to raise my daughter?"

"She's *our* daughter, and if you love her like you say you do, you'll listen to me. I've already pulled her back from the brink—*twice*. She's heading down a very dangerous path, Cal. If you let her out of your sight, you'll lose her."

"Since when are you in any position to be giving parental advice? You abandoned that child before she could even write your name."

Lada just shrugs, refusing to be shamed by Cal. "I did you both a favor. Hate me for it, if you want. I don't honestly care. I'm telling you she's in trouble, and I can't protect her anymore."

"Anymore? When did you *ever* look out for that child?"

"I kept my distance—I never tried to interfere in your lives." Lada nods toward Sachi. "I let you remarry."

"*Let* me? We had to have you declared dead!"

"I wanted you to. And I promise I'll disappear again once you do this one thing for me. Just take her away, Cal. That's all I ask." Lada leans in closer and practically whispers her next words. "You don't want her turning out like me, do you?" The way she says it makes it sound more like a threat than a warning. "If you let her out of your sight, they'll take her. I'm not kidding, Cal. They'll claim her and there won't be a damn thing that you or I can do about it."

Cal doesn't have a comeback this time but Sachi's about to lose it. "I don't understand—*who* is after her?"

Lada sighs and puts both of her hands on Sachi's shoulders. "The League. I work for them. I work miles and miles underground—in the deep. I have…a special ability. Nyla's got it too. That's why the League is trying to recruit her."

"Recruit her—to work for them? Underground?"

"Deep underground. It's important work but it's no life for a girl Nyla's age. Get her out of Brooklyn—maybe up to the Catskills. Keep her up there for a while and I'll see if I can buy her some time—"

Cal scoffs at Lada. "That's your plan? Go up into the mountains and wait?"

"It's your only option, Cal. This isn't some foreign enemy you can bomb to smithereens. We're fighting a war that's bigger than anything you could ever imagine."

"We?"

"The League."

"'The League.' You need your head checked. My daughter's not going anywhere. She's perfectly safe here with me." Cal pushes past Lada and opens the front door.

"Don't do this, Cal. Please, don't do this." Lada appeals to Sachi. "You love Nyla, I know you do. Don't let him throw her future away."

"I've heard enough. Why don't you do what you do best, *Lada*? Leave—and don't come back."

Lada drops Sachi's hand and walks out the front door without a backward glance. Without a goodbye. Cal closes the door and turns the two locks.

"I told you to go to your room, young lady."

I get up from my perch on the stairs. It looks like the show's over. Cal runs his hands over his shaved head and goes into the parlor. Sachi looks at me.

"Go upstairs, Nyla," she says loud enough for Cal to hear. Then she lowers her voice and adds, "Pack a bag—just in case."

For once, I do as I'm told without asking questions. I pull my knapsack out of the closet and take only the essentials out of my drawers: underwear, socks, t-shirts, a hoodie, cargo pants, and a pair of tights. Then I go to my desk and grab a compact flashlight. My phone and my Swiss army knife are already in my pocket. Before long I hear Sachi running up the stairs. I go out into the hallway and watch as she pulls a small carry-on bag out from under her bed and fills it as fast as she can. When she realizes I'm standing in the doorway Sachi says, "Go to bed, Nyla. But be ready to go first thing in the morning."

I nod, say goodnight, and then go into my room and close the door. Cal comes up a few minutes later. They aren't yelling anymore but I can tell my parents are still arguing about me. I expect to stay awake all night but before long my eyes start to close as the events of this crazy day take their toll. Falling asleep feels like falling into the deep. Cool, black shadows swallow me and extinguish every trace of anger, fear, and anxiety.

I sleep without dreams and wake at dawn to the sound of mourning doves cooing on the window ledge. I feel a strange sense of peace and for the first time in months, I feel like I know exactly what I need to do—who and where I need to be. I grab my phone and check my messages, knowing Keem's the only person who'll get a response. I think about updating my Facebook status to reassure everyone else, but can't come up with anything that won't lead to a bunch of annoying questions and comments. I try, "Starting a new a journey," but know my friends will ask about the destination and right now I haven't got a clue where I'll end up. So I replace it with, "Finally found my path." It sounds a bit hokey but at least it's not literal. And yet it's true. They can interpret it however they want, or just hit "like" and move on.

I want to call Keem—it would help a lot to hear his voice right now—but he spends Saturday mornings at the mosque learning Arabic. Plus it's early and I don't want him to start his day worrying about me. Sometimes I feel like that's all I bring to his life—a lot of stress and aggravation. It might be better this way. It might be better for everyone if I just disappeared for a while.

It takes a long time for me to write just a short message to Keem. I write things I never had the courage to say before but when I'm done, I can't bring myself to hit send. I save it to my draft folder instead and then take a long shower to clear my mind. I change into clean clothes, shoulder my knapsack, and head downstairs to find Sachi in the kitchen wrapping hot breakfast sandwiches in foil. "Have some juice," she says with a forced smile that barely hides her nervous state. "We'll eat on the road."

I accept the glass of cranberry juice Sachi hands me and wander down the hallway looking for Cal. I find him standing in the foyer, staring out the window, his hands jammed uselessly in his pockets. Sachi comes up the hallway and hands me the bag filled with fruit, bottles of water, and sandwiches for the road.

Cal turns and looks at her. "You're being irrational, Sachi. You're playing right into that woman's hands. She *wants* you to panic."

Sachi heaves her own bag onto her shoulder and takes the car keys off the hook on the wall. "I don't have time to rehash this, Cal. Lada has no reason to lie."

"Lie? You're assuming she even knows the difference between a lie and the truth. Emma was always…high strung."

"Well, leaving town for a while can't hurt. And maybe—just maybe—it'll help." Sachi goes up on her tiptoes to press a kiss on Cal's cheek. "I'll call you from the road." Then she opens the front door and heads for the car.

I go out the front door after her but stop and turn to look back at my father. As always, Cal looks totally unfazed. I raise my hand to wave goodbye but suddenly I feel the need to say something. I want to say, "Sorry I've been such a pain in the ass. Sorry I didn't turn out like you hoped." I want to say, "I love you, Daddy." But then my throat tightens and all that comes out is, "See you later, Cal."

He rattles the change in his pockets and forces a smile. "Take care of your mother, Nyla. She's pretty shook up."

I nod and hope the tears blurring my vision don't make me fall down the stoop stairs. I get in the car and take a deep breath. *I can do this.*

Sachi waits for me to fasten my seat belt and then pulls away from the curb. She drives toward Flatbush Avenue. It's the quickest way to get to the bridge—and to get out of the city.

"Hungry?" she asks.

"A little."

"Grab one of those bagels. I made yours with egg and cheese

only. Mine has bacon."

"Thanks." I stopped eating pork when Keem and I started to get close. When I told Cal he freaked out. He thought I was going to convert to Islam and start wearing a burqa. But Sachi didn't miss a beat and didn't make a fuss. "When you love someone, giving things up doesn't really feel like a sacrifice," she said.

I unwrap my sandwich and force myself to take a big bite. Eating saves me from having to talk, which is good since I'm this close to falling apart. I think of all the things Sachi has done for me over the years, the way she always introduces me as her daughter, no matter how confused people are. The way she almost always takes my side whenever I have a fight with Cal. The way she's reshaping her life to make this move to Brooklyn work for everyone. I reach for a bottle of water to help me get this food down. When I'm sure I can trust myself to sound normal I say, "I love you, Mom."

We're idling at a stoplight. Sachi takes her right hand off the steering wheel and cups my face in her small hand. "I love you, too, sweetheart."

I try to blink the tears out of my eyes but they fill up within a second or two. I give myself until Atlantic Avenue—four blocks from where we are now. "I think I'll save this for later," I say, wrapping up the uneaten half of my sandwich. I put it back in the bag Sachi packed, not my knapsack, though I know I'll be hungry later on. I take a few more sips of water and then set the bottle in the holder between our seats. With my left hand I grip the strap of my knapsack, keeping my right hand on the handle of the door. Then I realize I still have to unfasten my seatbelt.

Sachi sighs. "Where did all this traffic come from? It's not even nine o'clock."

I look ahead to the next stoplight and decide that's when I'll make my move. "There's construction up at Atlantic because of the new sports arena."

"Oh, right. How could I forget that eyesore?" Sachi looks around at the bustling avenue. "It feels like we're part of a mass exodus. I guess everybody's trying to get away this weekend." She smiles at me and I smile back. The light up ahead turns orange. There are five cars in front of ours and at least three behind.

"I think you'll like the hotel I picked. They have these private cabins that circle the lake. We can go hiking, canoeing, or we can just lounge by the pool. The food's supposed to be really good, too—they hired a top chef from one of those TV shows. I can't remember his name..."

My heart's racing but I bop my head to the tune playing on the radio. "I love that song," I say. "Can we turn it up?"

"Sure." Sachi reaches over and turns up the volume.

The light is red. I have less than a minute before it turns green. "I'm sorry, Sachi." I say the words out loud even though I know the music drowns out the sound of my voice. I take a deep breath, unclick my seatbelt, and yell, "I'm sorry, Mom!" Then I fling open the door and take off.

"Nyla!"

I run back up Flatbush Avenue as fast I can, heading for Grand Army Plaza. Everything around me is a blur—the people, the cars, the storefronts. My heart aches but not from running uphill. I betrayed Sachi and all she ever did was try to help me. I have to get off Flatbush before Sachi manages to turn the car around. She loves me too much to just let me go.

I turn off the busy avenue and slow to a walk so I attract less attention. I need a guide to get back to the deep, but Osiris got tasered the last time he tried to help me. And even if he hasn't given up on me, I don't know how or where to find him. I circle Grand Army Plaza, hoping to catch a glimpse of Osiris but he's nowhere to be found. Finally I go against the lights, dodge oncoming cars, and manage to get inside the plaza. I pass the bust of JFK and Neptune lounging in his fountain to make my way over to the giant arch.

It's a beautiful summer day. A steady stream of people is flowing under the arch as folks leave or head toward the farmer's market at the entrance to Prospect Park. I scan the plaza for a tall black man wearing cataract glasses but Osiris isn't here—or doesn't want to be found. I look across the lanes of traffic to the library. Then I think about the elevator buried beneath my feet. Could I find a way to open the locked door on the side of the arch? Could I work the elevator on my own?

"You look like you could use a guide."

I spin around and find Osiris standing behind me. He isn't smiling and I wonder if I should apologize for what happened last night. But it was Lada who tasered him so his beef should be with her, not me.

"I was afraid I wouldn't be able to find you," I say.

"It's my job to find *you*," Osiris says with a hint of a smile. He pulls a key from his pocket. "Are you sure you're ready for this?"

My stomach is twisting with hunger and my heart is aching over what I just did to Sachi. But I lie and say, "I'm ready," and we head back into the deep.

7.

Before the elevator begins its descent Osiris turns to me and says, "There seems to be some...confusion between you and Lada. It might help if you stated your intentions directly to her so that your mother knows that this is your choice."

That's not a conversation I really want to have right now but it isn't fair to let Osiris take the blame for my decision. When Lada sees me with him, she might flip out again. Of course, when I tell her this is what *I* want, she'll probably just direct all that anger at me. Osiris presses the code into the operating panel and I hold on as the elevator plunges into the deep.

When the doors open we head down a long, dark tunnel that leads to the same cavern we were in yesterday. Lada is working on the far side of the cavern but her attention is drawn by the rays of white light streaming from the lamps on our hard hats. Osiris stops and says, "I'll wait for you here."

I take a deep breath and cross the rocky terrain that separates me from Lada. She's prodding the ground with a long wooden pole and doesn't stop even when I get within a few feet of her. I wait for her to start something but she just ignores me and keeps on working. I feel a familiar scratchiness at the back of my throat as my nervousness changes to anger. "It was my choice," I say finally.

Lada keeps on poking the ground but turns so that her back is to me.

My throat starts to burn but I vow not to lose my temper.

"Cal didn't believe you but Sachi did. She tried to take me out of the city—"

Lada cuts me off. "But you ran away to join this damn circus. All that crap you said to me last night—trying to make me feel guilty for walking out on you. Well, you take a moment, Nyla, and think about what your stepmother's going through right now. Think about how it feels to be the one who's left behind."

My mouth falls open and for a moment I can't think of a single thing to say. The burning in my throat worsens and it feels like the air's being squeezed out of my lungs. "*You* said they would come for me. What's the point in running if—"

Lada holds her hand up to silence me. "You know what? Just get away from me. I can't even stand to look at you right now."

Then she turns her back on me again, leaving me standing there like a shunned beggar. Humiliated, I stomp back to where Osiris is standing. "Is she always such a bitch?"

"Give her time," he says. "She'll get used to the idea." Osiris pauses. "The decision to embark on this journey was yours to make, Nyla, not hers. But Lada is your mother—and a senior member of The League. Enemies and grudges are a luxury we can't afford here in the deep."

"You two don't exactly get along," I remind him.

"Not always. But we have learned to set aside our differences when necessary. The enemy feeds upon strife. Unity is our only hope."

A sharp laugh comes from behind us and we both turn to see the young white woman from yesterday sneering at us. She gives me the once over before asking Osiris, "What is this—bring your daughter to work day?"

"Roan, allow me to present Nyla, our newest recruit."

I don't know why Osiris is acting so formal when she's clearly making fun of him. I decide not to bother offering her my hand and fight the urge to flip her the bird instead. One member of The League's already pissed off at me—I don't need two.

Roan puts her hands on her hips and says, "So, you're the one causing all this *strife*. I sure hope she's worth it."

Roan directs her last words at Osiris but it's clear she's trying to get to me. I watch her swagger over to Lada and say something that causes both women to bust out laughing. Then Roan disappears down another tunnel and Lada goes on acting like I don't exist.

Osiris clears his throat and sounds more than a little embarrassed. "Don't mind Roan," he says. "She's a little testy these days. It's grief, really. We lost some people in Japan."

"Lost as in you can't find them?"

"No. They fell, Nyla. Cairene was one of the unlucky ones. She was...special to Roan."

"Special how? Were they in love?"

Osiris frowns. "I don't know. I try to mind my own business when it comes to affairs of the heart. But they were very close. Part of the same cohort—they joined The League at about the same. They went through a lot together."

"What happened in Japan?"

Osiris looks at me hard to make sure I'm for real. "There was a massive 9.0 earthquake there in March. It triggered a tsunami and a nuclear meltdown at the Fukushima plant."

My face flushes and I hope that the darkness will hide my embarrassment. The disaster in Japan happened around the same time as our adventure with Nuru last spring. We often talked about the earthquake at home because Sachi still has relatives in Japan, though she and her siblings were born in California. "I know about that but—" I take a deep breath so I don't sound so flustered. "I mean, what's that got to do with The League?"

Osiris watches me for a moment before taking my arm and

leading me over to a section of the cavern that's been marked with bits of neon pink tape.

"Do you know why we're here, Nyla—in New York?"

I try to think of a sensible answer but can't come up with anything so I shake my head.

"The League's members are largely gifted with intuitive abilities. They can sense imbalances and even subtle shifts in energy. But there are some of us who operate within the more traditional scientific fields—like seismology. Do you know what that is?"

"The study of earthquakes."

"Right. Our data indicate that New York will soon experience mild seismic activity."

A short laugh escapes my mouth. "An earthquake—in New York?"

"Don't laugh," Osiris says in a tone of voice that wipes the smile off my face. "Imagine the damage an earthquake could do in such a densely populated area."

I sober up. "I know, but—has there ever been an earthquake here? This isn't California."

"No, it's not, and New York doesn't sit on an active fault line. Nonetheless, the east coast does experiences earthquakes. They simply occur at such low magnitude that they are hardly noticed above ground. Our sensors have detected the potential for significant seismic activity farther south in Virginia, which may trigger an unexpected release of malevolent energy here in New York."

"Malevolent energy?" I pause and measure my words carefully. "Are you talking about—"

"Evil." Osiris takes a moment to gauge my response. I feel an irrational urge to laugh out loud again but manage to keep a straight face. Osiris must approve of my reaction because he continues. "Even minor seismic shifts can release energy that has been trapped deep in the earth for thousands of years. Should this energy reach the earth's surface, the results could be disastrous. The League surveys locations before and after seismic activity occurs. We detect fissures through which malevolent energy can be released. Your mother is what we call a presser."

"A presser." I take a moment to think this through. "Because she's able to push the bad energy back down?"

Osiris grants me an approving nod. "When a fissure is detected," he points at the pink tape stuck on the cave wall, "Lada uses her ability to suppress the rising energy and reseal the bedrock."

"Am I going to be a presser too?"

Osiris turns and leads me into the west tunnel. "That will be up to Marta."

I wonder how Marta decides which role each member of The League will play. It seems likely that I would be trained as a presser since I seem to have inherited whatever "gift" Lada possesses. I'm lost in my own thoughts and treading carefully on the uneven ground when Roan sprints past us, nearly knocking me down.

"Hey! Watch where you're going," I mutter angrily.

Roan ignores me and rushes on. When she reaches the cavern she calls out, "We've got a leak!"

Lada responds immediately, stopping just long enough to ruin the moment for me. "Get her out of here, Siris. Marta's losing patience with you."

"I'm not the only one who has trouble following orders from Marta," he replies.

"Clear out, Siris," Lada says in a menacing tone. "You can give the kid a tour some other time. Right now we have work to do." Lada doesn't even bother to look at me before heading down the tunnel after Roan.

Osiris takes my arm and we head back the way we came. "Let's go. Marta's waited long enough to meet you."

I look back in the direction Roan and Lada went. "Could I

watch them—just for a minute?"

Osiris frowns. Then he reaches up and turns a small dial on the wide arm of his cataract glasses. He stares down the tunnel as if he's taking some sort of measurement. I can't hear or see anything dangerous in this darkness but it must be safe because Osiris presses his fingers into my back and pushes me forward.

"It should be alright—just for a minute," he says. "You've never seen your mother at work, have you?"

Osiris sounds like he's proud of Lada and wants to show off her abilities. For some reason that makes me feel proud, too. I don't know anything about her but if others respect Lada, I feel like I should, too. Then I feel a stab of anger as I realize that Osiris and Roan know my own mother better than I do.

The west tunnel leads to a much smaller cavern. Its walls are made up of jagged hunks of black rock and the ground is even more treacherous. Roan is standing in a far corner, her eyes scrutinizing the overhanging rock as if she expects something to drop down at any moment. Lada's slowly pacing the uneven ground, holding her long wooden pole like she's about to spear a fish. Both women are still wearing their hard hats but the lamps on them have been turned off. Osiris reaches up and turns the lamp on my hat off before doing the same to his.

In a low voice Roan suddenly says, "There." She points up at what looks like a piece of that pink tape fluttering strangely in the still air. Lada lowers her rod and unlike the rest of us, glues her eyes to the ground. She doesn't look up even when the twitchy pink fragment begins to multiply—within seconds the dark cavern is filled with dancing bits of vibrant color! It feels like being in a sack full of butterflies. I creep forward, drawn into the astonishing scene. How will Lada and Roan "press" so many frenetic fragments of energy back into the hard rock beneath our feet?

Roan places a hand on her chest before closing her eyes and

bowing her head.

"Is she praying?" I ask.

Osiris shakes his head. "She's reading the energy in this space, tracing it to its source." Osiris has to pull me away. "Come," he says gently. "Marta's waited long enough."

I switch my lamp back on and follow Osiris down the tunnel, turning my head more than once to catch one last glimpse of the rosy glow. "I didn't think evil—malevolent energy—could be so…beautiful."

"The colorful, dispersed form is meant to distract and confuse. With the proper training, a presser can shape the energy—mold it into a more manageable form." Osiris sees the impression his words have made on me and goes on. "A mind gripped by fear is a presser's worst enemy. Malevolent energy can seize your thoughts and assume the shape of every demon from your worst nightmares. Roan and Lada have learned to empty their minds."

That stops me in my tracks. "Wait a minute. Are you saying this energy will become whatever you happen to be thinking about—whatever you fear most?"

"*The world for man with all it may contain is only what is compassed by the mind*. That applies most especially here in the deep."

The words echo faintly in my mind. "That's on the front of the library—above the door."

Osiris nods. I open my mouth to ask another question but he suddenly raises his hand to stop me. I wait anxiously as Osiris reaches up to adjust the dial on his glasses. He frowns, looks back down the tunnel and says, "Wait here." Then he breaks into a run and disappears, leaving me alone in the dark.

I can hear yelling coming from the cavern. I want to do as I'm told but find myself irresistibly drawn to the soft pink glow at the end of the tunnel. I creep along, touching the side of the tunnel to reassure myself. I reach the mouth of the cavern just as Roan yells,

"Look out!"

I watch breathlessly as Lada jumps back and narrowly escapes being crushed by a falling hunk of rock.

"It's moving up," Osiris shouts. "Pin it down, Lada. Pin it down!"

How can she? I think to myself. The pretty dancing butterflies are gone and the cavern is now filled with worm-like creatures that appear to be feasting on the darkness itself. Lada swings her pole and with each stroke the pink worms seem to flock to her—it's like watching the guy at Coney Island whip up a cone of cotton candy. Lada swings her wooden pole in a wide arc and the pink worms cling to the rod. A swipe of black space is left behind but within seconds more pink worms surge forward, surrounding her completely. Osiris has his hand on the dial by his left eye. He's scanning the cavern, trying to see through the pink swarm. "There's another source—"

But before he can point it out to Lada and Roan there's an eerie groan from below followed by a thunderous roar. The floor of the cavern rumbles and then splits apart in a massive explosion that lifts Roan and Osiris off their feet and slams them into the jagged walls of the cave.

I scream—I *think* I scream—but it's hard to hear over the rising buzz of energy that's filling the cavern. I enter the cave and scramble over the jagged rocks to reach Osiris. His broken leg is twisted beneath his body and he doesn't respond when I shake him and call his name. I make my way over to Roan next. Blood is oozing from a deep gash above her ear. She isn't unconscious but she can't seem to stand and I can't understand the slurred words coming out of her mouth.

"What do I do?" I shout the words but Lada doesn't seem to hear me. She's still swinging at the wriggling pink worms but there are too many for her to handle on her own. Soon they will overwhelm her—she cannot "pin" them down and seal the two fissures by herself. I haven't been trained yet but there must be *something* I can do. I don't plan to enter The League by watching my own mother "fall."

A gaping chasm separates me from Lada. The malevolent energy that first entered the small space at a trickle is now pouring into the cavern and its focus seems to be Lada. A few stray worms have settled on Osiris and are working their way toward his open mouth. Roan has enough strength left to swat at the ones clinging to her bloody face. Lada is pinned against the far wall of the cavern and it's clear her strength is failing. As the worms press forward she falls to one knee and must use her rod to push herself back up on two feet.

I have to reach Lada. I get as close as I can to the edge of the abyss and yell, "Tell me what to do!"

I'm not sure how to explain what happens next. Lada opens her mouth for just a couple of seconds, shouting, "Go! Just GO!" And suddenly the worms are no longer worms—they merge into some sort of giant amoeba-like creature. It folds itself around Lada's body, pries open her jaw, and begins pouring itself down her throat.

I want to run. I want to close my eyes, open them again, and be standing above ground with the August sun shining on my face. But right now I can't even move. I look down and find both my feet are mired in some kind of sludge. I stood on solid rock just a moment ago but now I'm stuck, forced to watch this *thing* suck the life out of my mother. At least I think that's what it's doing—Lada's head is tilted back and she has dropped to her knees. The wooden pole is still in her hands but her arms hang limply at her side.

"Lada! LADA!" If she can hear me she shows no sign. I scream at the *thing* instead. "Leave her alone—get away from her!"

I yell until I feel the fire sizzling at the base of my throat. *Someone help me*. The words slip through my lips like steam but there is no one left to hear them. I cast a desperate glance at Osiris and Roan. Without them what can I do? My throat begins to close as if what's happening to Lada is happening to me. And I'm sure it *will* happen to me next unless I figure out a way to break free.

I tug at my legs but it's as if my feet are encased in cement. I don't want to watch but I force myself to witness everything that's happening to Lada. The giant amoeba changes color, turning into a lurid, yellow blob that looks like it's trying to suck something out of my mother. It is pulsing with life—*her* life. A thread of blue light leaves Lada's mouth and winds through its sheer body, throbbing like a vein. The wooden pole falls from Lada's hands and clatters to the ground.

Every part of me is shaking with rage except for my feet, which are glued to the ground. I will *not* let this happen. After more than a decade of missing my mother—ten years of dreaming about her and all the things she could do to make it up to me—I finally found her three miles underground. And now, before Lada has a chance to make amends, before she could get to know the kind of person I've become, this disgusting *thing* is trying to take her away again. I know I am close to losing control. My blood is boiling and it's getting hard to breathe, which is just how I felt when Osiris snatched D off the train. It was Keem who reined me in then but this time I am alone. I have to do this on my own. *I have to.*

I feel a wave of nausea rising within me but when I open my mouth to puke, only hot sound heaves out of me. The force of my own voice throws my head back and I yell in a way I have never yelled before. When my voice finally gives out I lean forward, panting as if I've just run a marathon. My helmet falls off and clatters into the abyss. *I can do this.* I grip my knee and try to lift my left leg. Nothing. I take a deep breath and try again, this time while tipping my head up at the blackness above and yelling as hard as I can. Both my ears pop and a scary rumbling comes from below but my left foot slowly slides out of its sludge tomb. I'm halfway free!

I look over at Lada and hope that she can hold on a bit longer. I don't know how I'll cross the chasm to reach her but for now I focus on freeing my right foot. The long blue thread glows inside the giant amoeba, filling the small cave with rippling shadows that make me feel like I'm underwater. I watch as it loosens its grip on my mother, letting her slump to the ground in a heap. Then it turns to me, its pale green mass trembling with—what? Rage? Desire? Lada lies motionless on the other side of the cavern. I hope that she is just unconscious. I hope that I am not too late. Certain that the green mass is somehow watching me, I bend over, grab my right knee, and manage to free my other foot with another deafening yell.

The mass leaves Lada's lifeless body and hovers over the chasm. I have its attention now but I don't know what to say or do next. It looms over me and sighs with a disgusting shudder of anticipation. Though it has no mouth I hear it speak to me: *You will exceed her in every way.*

What's that supposed to mean? I stand before it, my chest heaving, my throat raw, sweat sizzling on my hot skin. I don't know what to do. I don't know what I *can* do. I look past it—through it—at my mother, lying still on the ground. I'll never get to know her now.

"You killed her." It's all I can think to say. I hiss the accusation at the shapeless, murderous mass and blink away the tears filling my eyes. The mass drifts toward me, changing from an ugly green blob to a cloud of glittering silver dust. I remember what Osiris said about malevolent energy using a presser's thoughts to its advantage. I try to empty my mind but all I can think about is Lada—how she abandoned me as a kid and then did all she could to prevent me from joining The League. What is it about me that makes it so easy for her to walk away? I deserve better.

The silver mass has no limbs but I feel it wrapping me in a tender embrace. *You are so precious.* Its touch cools my feverish body and I feel my knees weaken—it would be so easy to give in, to let myself fall back into this soft, silver pillow. I wonder if this is how Lada felt before the blue thread was pulled out of her. If this is the end, it's not as bad as I imagined it would be. I close my eyes. If there is a heaven or an afterlife, maybe I'll find Lada again.

I cast a final glance at my mother. "Goodbye" is on the tip of my tongue but before I speak I see something that stuns me. Lada is no longer slumped over. She was on her knees when the mass finished with her and turned to me, but now she is crouched with her back against the wall of the cavern. Her head is titled upward but her eyes are closed. Lada's alive. My mother is alive. It's not too late!

"Lada!" I open my mouth for just a moment and suddenly it feels like a hundred cold fingers are prying my jaws apart. I draw back from the edge of the chasm and try to throw off the silver mass but find I am inside of it now. The dazzling silver sphere surrounds me in a stifling embrace. I stiffen against it and try to control my thoughts. I am no longer ready to surrender. Now I am ready to fight.

I think of Lada—I think of Keem and D and Cal and Sachi. I think of this mass devastating the people I love by consuming me. My body heats up and the cool, soothing touch of the mass turns abrasive as I struggle to break free.

"Get off me!"

You are mine.

I freeze for a second as my mind takes me back to that night in Germany. *Never again.* Fury replaces the feeling of panic and I will myself to act. If this thing really can read my thoughts then I shouldn't even need to speak. *I am* not *yours. I am my own, my own, my own.* I pull up the fire in my belly and spew it at the mass. "I said, GET OFF!"

Those words hurl me forward, and I almost choke on another wave of nausea. When I straighten, I find that my rage has all the volume it needs. I tip my head back and yell loud enough to wake the dead. The mass pulls back and shrinks into a cringing ball, cowed by my power. Then the air in the cavern changes and for the first time I sense the presence of evil. The mass crackles with hostility. Then it shatters into a column of tiny silver daggers and flings every last one at me.

I laugh. I *think* I laugh. I open my mouth and despite the excruciating pain suck every blade deep into my core. Even in its new form, I can tell the mass of malevolent energy is afraid of me. And to be honest, I'm scaring myself right now. The agony of a thousand razor blades sliding down my throat makes me giddy. I *am* laughing. I know it now. But I can't seem to stop. I feel like I am ten feet tall—far too big to fit inside this cavern, far too powerful to ever be frightened again. For the first time in my life I feel totally in control.

When the last dagger passes through my lips I open my eyes and scan the dark, empty cavern. Silence surrounds me and I shiver as what's left of the mass crystallizes inside of me. I feel like my throat is lined with diamonds. My blood slides through my veins like ice water. I have never felt so at peace.

I step closer to the edge of the chasm to get a better look at Lada. Her helmet is on the ground but its light still shines, sending up a narrow beam of white light. Lada is still in a crouching position but her head is now hanging down so low that her chin almost touches her chest. I call her name and watch with delight as my mother opens her eyes with a loud gasp. Using the wooden pole as a crutch, she manages to pull herself to her feet. Behind me I hear similar groans as Osiris regains consciousness and Roan summons the strength to stand.

I beam at my mother and wait for pride to wipe the worry from her face. But Lada says nothing as she takes a few tentative steps toward the edge of the chasm. She blinks over and over before putting a hand up as if to shield her eyes from some kind of glare. My mother is alive but she's acting like she doesn't even recognize me.

"Nyla?"

Something's wrong. Was the blue thread taken by the mass

somehow connected to her memory? I raise my hand and wave. "It's me, Lada." I don't sound like my usual self but I go on anyway. "Everything's going to be okay. I did it—I did it all by myself!"

I want her to be as proud of me as I am of myself, but Lada still looks confused. In fact, it seems like she can barely stand to look at me. I measure the chasm separating me from my mother and wonder if I could clear it. I *feel* like I could. I feel like I can do anything right now.

Lada turns away from me and drops the hand she was holding up to protect her eyes. I look down at my hands and realize the glare is coming from me—the cold silver blood in my veins is making me glow. I am radiant. I am beautiful!

But not to Roan. She calls out a warning as Lada prepares to cross the chasm. "Lada—don't! Stay away from her!"

I look over my shoulder and see Roan inching along the wall of the cavern, her blood-smeared face turned away from my brilliance. Lada has moved away from me, too. I watch as she walks to the far end of the chasm, judges the distance, and then uses her pole to launch herself into the air. She practically lands in Roan's desperate, outstretched arms.

"We can't let her surface, Lada—we can't!"

Roan's fear confuses me but I don't feel any anger towards her. I leave them huddled against the wall of the cavern and tend to Osiris instead. As I approach he quickly reaches for the dial on the side of his glasses.

"I'm not getting a reading!" He says this to them, not me.

I hold out my hand to help him up but Osiris shakes his head. "I can't. It's broken."

I glance down and see that his left leg is turned outward at an unnatural angle. "Hold still," I tell him. Then I reach down and trace my silver fingertips along his broken leg. Osiris grits his teeth and manages to not make a sound as the bones slowly realign.

When his leg extends in a straight line once more, I pull back and wait for him to catch his breath. Then I offer Osiris my hand again. "Ready?"

I can feel Roan and Lada standing behind me. I feel them watching me—judging me. I look into Osiris's face and see myself reflected in his dark lenses. The glow surrounding me has dimmed now that I've healed his leg. Osiris grips my hand and I pull him to his feet. His left leg is stiff but strong enough to support his weight. "Thank you," he says, suddenly shy. I nod and step back so I can face them all.

Lada glares at me but her voice is full of wonder. "What have you done?"

A moment ago I felt so powerful but now I feel like a naughty little girl. What have I done wrong? "I fixed his leg," I say cautiously.

"That's not what I mean and you know it!" she hisses.

I look at my mother and wonder why there is so much anger in her voice—and so much fear. "It's okay, Lada." I speak gently and reach out to touch her. I only want to reassure her, but Roan thrusts herself between us.

"The hell it is—I saw what you did!"

Lada is holding Roan around the waist, helping her to stand upright. I know my help is unwanted but I can't ignore her open wound. As I draw near, Roan pulls back. "Don't be afraid," I say in a voice that sounds more like my own. I reach for the gash above her ear and feel the scalp closing beneath my fingertips. "That's better." I smile to hide the sudden fatigue that washes over me. Roan opens her eyes and stares at me with a mixture of horror and awe.

Osiris takes my arm and pulls me back from the two women. "She's clean, Lada."

Lada shakes her head. "But that's impossible. How could she be clean after consuming a mass that size? We all should've been destroyed."

Osiris just shrugs. "As far as I know, nothing like this has ever happened before. But Marta knows the history of The League better than I do. A gift like that might not be news to her. My guess is that Nyla somehow managed to absorb *and* convert the energy."

I turn to my mother, thoroughly confused. "I thought you'd be happy. I mean, I know you don't think I'm ready for this, and I know I still have a lot to learn but…I saved us, Lada. I don't know how, but I did. Right?"

To my surprise, tears slide down Lada's cheeks, leaving clean tracks on her dirt-smeared skin. She sighs and swipes at her eyes with the back of her hand. When Lada looks at me again, her eyes are full of sorrow. "It's not too late for you to run, Nyla. I'll do whatever I can to help you get away."

Osiris frowns. "Lada, you know I can't allow you to do anything that would jeopardize—"

"Stay out of it, Siris!" she barks. "You of all people should know what her life will be like from now on. What they'll do to her once they know what she's capable of."

Osiris hangs his head and says nothing more. Lada places her hands on my shoulders and looks straight into my eyes. I have lost my glow completely but I don't care. This is the closest I have been to my mother since I was four years old.

"It won't be easy to deny The League," she says, "but it *can* be done."

My mind is racing. I don't want to say anything that will push my mother away. "But…this is where I belong. Here in the deep—with you."

In an instant I know that I have chosen the wrong words. Lada's hands fall away from my shoulders and she steps back, resigned.

Roan keeps her distance from me but says, "She belongs here alright. And we better keep her down here until Marta figures out what to do."

Lada's anger returns but this time it's directed at Roan. "We are *not* leaving her down here! *She* didn't leave *us*."

Roan sulks but says nothing more. I wish Lada would say my name instead of talking about me like I'm not here. Still, my mother defended me and it means a lot to know she's on my side.

"We'd better close this seam," Osiris says finally. "Are you strong enough, Roan?"

"Of course, I am," she snaps. "But are you sure that's what you want me to do?" Roan can barely bring herself to look at me. "I mean, what if this is some kind of trick? Maybe she's just a vehicle—it could be using her to get above ground!"

Osiris sighs impatiently. "I told you—*she's clean*. Now close the seam, Roan."

The white girl scowls at me, then makes a sound of disgust and heads over to the edge of the chasm. Osiris signals for me to follow him. We stand at the mouth of the tunnel and watch as Roan and Lada prepare to cut off the passage through which the malevolent energy entered the cavern. Roan places a hand on her chest and bows her head for a moment. Then she spreads her arms wide as if she were nailed to a cross. Lada stands at the far end of the cavern, her wooden pole pressed firmly into the rocky floor. Without saying a word, Roan opens her eyes and brings her hands together in a resounding clap. Then she flings her arms apart once more and this time brings them together slowly—so slowly that for a moment I can't even tell that her arms are moving. But they are and so is the ground. The rock beneath Roan's feet groans, shifts, and slowly seals itself shut.

Osiris adjusts the dial on his glasses before going back into the cavern. He scans the seam and assures them that he can no longer detect any leaks. I watch as Lada prods at the rocky floor with her pole, not seeming to trust Osiris' report. Roan clutches her chest and takes a few wobbly steps toward Lada. She nearly faints but Osiris catches her in time.

"Don't worry," he says, "I got you."

"Where's Nyla?"

I hear Lada's voice but it sounds like she is on a distant shore while I am being washed out to sea. I reach for the wall of the tunnel, hoping to steady myself, but the wall is no longer there. I feel the strength draining out of my limbs. There is no one to catch me when I fall.

8.

I hear before I can see. My eyes refuse to open but I can sense two people standing over me, whispering angrily.

"So—what is she?"

"What's that supposed to mean? She's just a kid, Roan. The only thing special about her is that she happens to be *my* kid."

"Give it a rest, Lada. I was *there*. I saw what she did. She's not one of us."

"Shut up, Roan!"

"You really think you can keep something like this from Marta?"

Lada changes her tone from menacing to pleading. "Listen, Roan. I've already talked to Osiris. He promised he wouldn't say anything to her until I had a chance to work out some kind of arrangement—"

"Get real, Lada. Why do you think they went after your kid in the first place? They *know*. I bet they've known all along."

There is a long pause. I lie still and try to read the silence between Lada and Roan. Finally my mother says, "I'm not giving her up without a fight."

Roan sighs. "This is bigger than you, Lada. The League needs her. What Nyla can do—if she really can convert mal-N—it changes everything."

"It changes *nothing*! They'll just use her the same way they use us."

Lada walks out of the room, taking with her some of my energy. I let my weary body sink like a coin tossed into a fountain and sleep soundly for what seems like days. When I open my eyes again I feel something soft and cool pressing into my skin. I reach up to see what it is and the hand holding the damp cloth withdraws.

"You're back." Roan almost smiles at me. Her long black braid hangs over her shoulder like a snake.

I squint in the dim light. The sun has set and the room would be pitch black but for a small lamp in the far corner. Roan is seated next to me on a narrow bed. An identical bed is just a few feet away, pushed up against a bare wall. I had hoped it was my mother nursing me but try not to show my disappointment. "Where's Lada?" I ask with what's left of my voice. My throat feels like I swallowed a cheese grater.

"Down the hall—with Marta." Roan sets the cloth and basin aside. "Can you sit up?"

I press my feet into the mattress and slide myself up against the headboard. My skull throbs for a moment and I shut my eyes to erase the dizziness. "Water, please."

Roan hands me a glass from the nightstand and watches as I drain it in three long gulps. "Better?"

I open my eyes and realize that I do feel better. The pounding and the dizziness are gone, though I still flinch when she turns on a second lamp next to the bed.

"Sorry. I need to see what I'm doing."

I glance at the pointy pliers in her hand and pull back. "What *are* you doing?"

"Relax." Roan reaches up and pushes my hair out of my face. "Marta says your piercings have to come out."

"Why?"

Roan looks at me for a moment and then gets up from the bed. She takes a small hand mirror off a nearby dresser and passes it to me.

I look at my reflection and gasp. There is a thin silver dagger embedded in my chin where my piercing—a silver ball—used to be. Two other silver droplets rest like tears by my temple. "Who did this to me?"

Roan frowns. "*You* did. Some of your piercings melted when you…tried to help your mother."

"Melted?"

"You didn't feel it? It must have hurt like hell." Roan sits down again and reaches for my face. "The rings shouldn't be a problem. But your chin—and here," she touches the tender spot near my left temple. "It looks like those are permanent."

"Permanent?"

"Metal isn't recommended. There can be problems with conductivity." She looks at me and sees my confusion. "Too much heat—the energy passing through your body melted the metal into your skin. If you sit real still I'll try to cut these rings along your brow."

"And my earrings?" I've got more than half a dozen silver rings in each of my ears.

"Those will have to go, too."

"What about the ear plugs? They're not metal."

Roan stares at me without emotion. "You really want to take that chance?" She brings the pliers up to my face and I try not to flinch as she snips each ring and then gently slides it out of my skin.

While Roan works I play with my hands, turning all of my rings to ensure that they're not welded together or fastened to my fingers. The silence between us makes the moment uncomfortably intimate. I wonder if Roan is simply following orders or if she's changed her mind about me.

Finally I ask, "Why are you doing this?"

Roan snips another ring along my outer ear, slides it out, and hands it to me. "Think you could do this on your own?"

"No. But you didn't want anything to do with me before. You even told them to leave me down there!"

Roan looks at the bare, beige wall instead of looking at me. She sighs and says, "What happened this morning—it was intense, alright? I probably said some things I shouldn't have." She tries to resume her work but that's not enough of an answer for me. I push the pliers away and force her to look at me.

"I heard what you said to Lada. You think I'm a freak!"

"You *are* a freak, kid. But so am I. The League wouldn't want us if we were normal." She swallows her pride and adds, "I'm sorry, alright? I just figured one good turn deserves another. You fixed me up, remember?" Roan tosses her braid over her shoulder so I can see the healed wound above her ear.

I can't think of anything else to say and figure I have to trust her—for now. I lean back against the headboard and Roan leans in again with the pliers. When she's done extracting all my piercings, I pull my eight rings off my fingers and hand over all but one.

Roan surveys each silver band and nods approvingly. "Opal, jade, garnet, turquoise. Looks like you were fully armed."

"What do you mean?"

"These semi-precious stones aren't worth a lot up here but they're very powerful in the deep."

"Why?" I bought those rings because they were pretty, not powerful.

Roan groans. "Marta's better at explaining all this. Let's just say that in the deep gemstones are *home*, in a way. Closer to their source."

I want to ask another question but get distracted by the beautiful amber ring in my hand—the one ring I can't surrender. I touch the dagger embedded in my chin and wonder what Keem would say if he could see me now. I wonder when I'll see him again. "A friend gave this to me. I can't wear it anymore?"

Roan smirks but manages not to laugh at me. "Your *friend* has good taste."

I can tell she's not the sentimental type. I don't want her to know how I feel about Keem but then I feel ashamed for hiding my feelings. Keem never hides how he feels about me.

"You can keep the stone," she says. "Just change the setting." Roan pulls a dazzling amethyst amulet from inside her t-shirt. "I use leather for mine. It's durable, soft. Safer than silver or gold."

I reach out and touch the large purple stone, realizing that's what she was clutching in the deep. "It's beautiful. Was it a gift?"

She nods. "To myself. Most of us need a source object—something from the natural world to help focus our energy. Lada uses core wood. Cypress, I think, or baobab."

"You mean that pole she was swinging around?"

Roan nods. "Not many of us use wood but Lada prefers it. I don't know why. She's kind of old school, I guess."

I pull back my fingers and Roan slips the amethyst back inside her shirt. I hear a door slam somewhere in the apartment, which prompts me to ask, "Is Lada in trouble?"

Roan frowns. "Trouble? Why would you think that?"

"You said she was talking to Marta. I don't want to make things difficult for her."

Roan shakes her head and gives me a genuine smile. "Don't worry about it, kid. Marta's probably going to give Lada a medal—or a nice long vacation—for bringing you into the fold."

I look around the room. The walls are bare, the furnishings simple. There's nothing that feels like home. "Lada doesn't want me here."

Roan presses her thin lips into a colorless seam. I appreciate that she takes the time to find words that will make this easier for me. "She wanted a different life for you, Nyla. But some things are beyond our control."

We sit in silence for a moment. I look up when I realize Roan is staring at me. "What?" The word comes out with a bit more attitude than I intended.

Roan gets up off the bed. "Nothing. I'll go get some rubbing alcohol—you don't want to risk an infection." She sweeps the broken studs and rings off the nightstand and into her palm. I reach up and touch the holes left in my face. I look in the hand mirror and barely recognize myself.

Roan watches me and gently rests a hand on my shoulder. "You're so young."

I don't look at her but I hear the pity in her voice. I don't need her sympathy but when I look at my own reflection I know that she's right. I look like a little kid—like the girl I used to be. The girl who couldn't take care of herself.

Without looking away from the mirror I ask, "How old were you when—when you..."

"I was sixteen when I figured out something wasn't right. They came for me a year later."

I lift my eyes to scan her face. "How old are you now?"

"Nineteen."

I try but fail to hide my surprise.

"It ages you," she says.

"What does?"

I shiver as her fingertips trace my perforated brow. Looking at Roan is like looking at my future.

"Power," she says flatly before walking out of the room.

Somewhere in the apartment a door creaks open and the sound of raised voices drifts down the hall. I get out of bed and stick my head out the door. The hallway is dark but a slice of orange light comes from a door that is slightly ajar. I creep down the hall but stop a few feet from the open door and listen to the angry voices. Lada and Osiris are going at it again. If Marta's in the room, she doesn't seem to have much to say.

"We can't afford to let this opportunity slip away."

Lada appeals directly to her boss. "Give her two more years—fourteen is too young. You've said it yourself, Marta."

Osiris objects. "Nyla isn't like other recruits. Plus she's already had her awakening. It would be cruel to cast her out into the world now—in her condition."

Lada's temper flares. "Oh, please—like you care about 'her condition.' You think I don't know what you've got in store for her? You can't wait to stick a bunch of needles and tubes in her—you'd bleed her dry if it helped you get what you want."

I'm so busy eavesdropping that I don't see Roan until she is standing right next to me. She clamps a hand over my mouth to silence my surprise and drags me back down the hall.

"I—I need to use the bathroom."

"That wasn't it." Roan stares at me until I drop my gaze and look at the floor. "It's this way."

Roan leads me back down the hall, past the room where Lada and Osiris are arguing. She flicks on a bright fluorescent light and hands me the bottle of rubbing alcohol. Then she heads back down the hall without saying another word.

I close the door and splash some cool water on my face. Then I stare at my reflection in the mirror over the sink, trying to get used to the new me. I find some cotton balls in the cupboard under the sink and dab the alcohol on the many holes in my face. Aside from a few medical supplies, the bathroom is bare like my room. I wonder if The League only uses this apartment as a temporary dorm. I couldn't imagine living in such an impersonal place. I run a hand through my wild hair, taming it a bit. Then I take a deep breath, open the door, and go looking for my mother.

Roan is waiting for me at the far end of the hallway. I head toward her but as soon as I pass the room Lada's in, I kneel and pretend to lace up my boot.

Roan folds her arms across her chest and says one word. "Don't."

I stand up but stay near the open door. "Why not?" I whisper. "They're talking about me, right?"

Roan walks over and takes my arm. "Come on, the kitchen's this way. I'll make you something to eat."

"I'm not hungry."

"Then take a hint, Nyla," Roan hisses at me. "Your mother needs some privacy right now."

I look over my shoulder at the orange glow coming from the open door. "Fine," I finally say, unable to think of any alternative besides bursting into the room and demanding to know what's going on. That's not the kind of first impression I want to make on Marta.

Roan turns and leads the way down another, shorter hallway. I follow her but slowly so that I can hear a bit more of what's being said. Lada still sounds heated.

"It isn't fair. I gave her up once already—I gave her up to keep her safe!"

Finally I hear Marta's voice. She speaks softly but I think I can detect a Spanish accent. "You can't protect her anymore, Lada. All you can do is give her the tools she needs to manage her gift."

"It's not a *gift*. It's a curse!"

Suddenly the hallway fills with orange light as the door to the room is flung open. Lada storms down the hall but stops when she sees me. "You hungry?"

I avoid Roan's eyes and say, "A little." The truth is I'm starving.

"Let's go then."

Lada heads for the front door and I rush to keep up. We pass the bathroom and three more closed doors, which I assume are bedrooms. The hallway opens into a large, bare living room area with beige walls and beige carpet. I don't know who lives here but the place is spotless. Maybe Marta tidies up while the others are in the deep. I wonder when I'm going to meet my new boss but Lada looks too pissed to talk right now so I keep my mouth shut.

As we wait for the elevator I pull out my phone and check my messages.

Lada sees me and smirks. "Your folks call the police yet?"

"I doubt it."

"Well, make sure they don't. When we get back call them and let them know you're alright."

"Okay." I open a text from Keem and hit reply. Lada watches me, annoyed.

"What are you doing?"

"I'm just texting a friend."

"You don't have friends—not anymore. Put the phone away." I stare at her in disbelief but Lada just gets madder. "*Now,*" she snaps at me. I put my phone in my pocket before she can snatch it out of my hand.

We say nothing in the elevator but once we're outside and a few blocks away from the apartment, Lada seems to relax. "Listen, the next few weeks are going to be rough for you. I know our world must seem strange and it isn't easy cutting yourself off from the people you love. But you need to keep them at a distance right now. You can't commit to The League if you're holding onto the past."

"D and Keem already know about the deep."

Lada shakes her head. "They took an elevator ride. They have no idea what you're stepping into."

"They do! You saw D's hand, right—how it glowed underground? That's Nuru."

"Nuru?"

I fight the urge to tell Lada every last detail of our adventure in March. But instead I play it cool and say, "You're not the only one with stories to tell."

Lada's eyebrows go up. "Excuse me. Just tell them you need some space for the next little while." She watches me and must know what I think of her new rules. "I mean it, Nyla. Either you get them to back off or I'll get Liev to scare them off."

"Who's Liev?" I ask.

"The charming guy who snatched D yesterday."

That prick. I don't appreciate Lada threatening my friends. "Keem would fight for me," I warn her.

Lada just laughs. "So would the little one, I bet. But that's not what you need right now."

"Oh yeah? What do I need?"

Lada stops and pulls open the door of a pizzeria. "Food."

We each order the slice and soda combo and then take our trays to a table at the back. My face is still a bit sore from Roan's extractions but I'm too hungry to take dainty little bites. Lada eats without looking at or speaking to me. She wolfs down half her slice and then stops to look around at the other customers.

"Something wrong?" I ask.

Lada shakes her head, still managing to avoid eye contact with me. "I'd almost forgotten," she says softly.

"What?"

"How it feels to be normal."

For a moment I wonder if she ever wanted this—if she ever longed to sit across a table and eat with me. I have a hundred different questions swirling around my brain. I manage to pick one but can't quite look my mother in the eye. "Did they come for you the way they came for me?"

Lada takes another bite of pizza and grunts. "Pretty much."

"In Germany?"

She nods. "But it started before then. The League can be very...persuasive. And persistent."

"Are you saying you didn't have a choice?"

"No. In the end…I guess they just wore me down. My guide wouldn't go away and neither would the symptoms."

I take a sip of soda and try to steady my voice. "I started seeing things just after Christmas. I thought I was losing my mind."

Lada shows no sign of alarm or even sympathy. She just nods like what I've said makes perfect sense.

"Did you see things too?" I ask.

"No. But I lost…" Lada stops and then tries again. "It got so I couldn't touch things. Not without changing them in some way." She looks around the pizza joint until her gaze falls on a young father leaning across the table to wipe orange grease off his little girl's mouth. When he pulls the napkin away the child beams at him like the sun. *Two-fifty*, I think to myself. *All that joy for two-fifty*. Cal's face flits across my mind but I can't go there right now.

"I was afraid. I didn't know what was happening to me—what I might do to the people I loved." Lada shrugs. "So I left."

"And joined The League. Did they help you?"

Lada pulls her eyes away from the little girl and stares at the half-eaten slice on her paper plate instead. "They taught me how to redirect my energy."

"Away from me."

She looks at me then. "You've seen the deep. I couldn't exactly take you with me, Nyla. Which reminds me—are you on the Pill?"

I nearly choke on the mouthful of pizza I had been about to swallow. "What?"

"Birth control—you know what that is, right?"

"Of course, I do!" I hiss at her, hoping she'll lower her voice. "Not that it's any of your business."

"That's my blood in your veins—I'm making it my business."

I take a moment and try to remember the last time I got my period. I started early, before I was twelve, but a few months ago it stopped altogether and hasn't come back. I'm not about to tell *her* that, though. "I'm not sexually active, alright?"

Lada glances at the young father and little girl. "You will be soon, judging by the way your tall, dark, and handsome 'friend' looks at you."

"Keem isn't like that. And *he* doesn't decide when—*I* do."

Lada looks at me with something close to admiration. "I'm glad to hear that. It's clear that he likes you—he may even think he loves you. But he doesn't own you. Your body's your own, Nyla."

"I don't need you to tell me that." The venom in my voice even surprises me.

She watches me a moment longer and then asks quietly, "You learn the hard way?"

I hesitate and avoid her eyes. "Maybe."

Lada sucks the last of her soda through the straw and then crushes the can with one hand. "Did Cal make the little prick pay?"

I lift my chin and finally look at my mother. "*I* did. I split his head open."

Again Lada looks at me with a strange, sad sort of pride. She reaches out a hand and shifts my bangs out of my eyes, then gently touches the two silver teardrops at my temple. "Is that why you went punk—to scare the boys away?" She hurries on before I can protest. "Your father must have had a heart attack when you cut your hair. Cal was always so proud of his little long-haired princess."

I shrug and pretend that my mother's sudden tenderness hasn't unsettled me. "I couldn't be daddy's little girl forever. Besides, he's supposed to love me no matter what I look like."

Lada leans back and glances over at the father and daughter. "Love's never unconditional. There are always strings attached."

"Is that what I was—a string that tied you down?"

Lada says nothing for a moment. "I thought that if I mixed my blood with your father's—I could dilute it. I thought it would be ok."

She tries to laugh but can't. "And look at you now."

"You wish I'd never been born?"

Lada's fingers fly from the crumpled can to my bare wrist. "I never said that!" She glares at me for a long moment before letting go. "I just want you to think things through. If Marta's right about your abilities, then you need to think long and hard about what it might mean for you to reproduce."

I don't plan to have a whole bunch of kids—not now, maybe never. But I don't like being told what I can and cannot do so I decide to play devil's advocate. "What if that's the answer—making more and more freaks for The League. We could build our own army and end it once and for all."

Lada makes a sound of contempt. "You sound like Cal the war monger."

"I'm just saying there's strength in numbers. You don't have to save the world all by yourself."

"Oh yeah? Well, before you start popping out superbabies, think about how you'd feel watching one of your kids die before your eyes. Because it happens, Nyla. It almost happened to me today."

I stare at the pizza crust on my plate and quietly admit, "I wasn't sure you were going to make it. I saw it pull something out of you—like a glowing blue thread. Was that your memory?"

"It's more complicated than that. Marta will teach you about core energy tomorrow."

"How were you able to…come back?"

"Some of us have regenerative abilities." I watch in silent amazement as Lada traces her fingers along the creases in the crushed soda can, straightening the crumpled metal until the damage is undone. "I thought for sure my time was up. None of us wants to die but the worst part was knowing that if I fell, you'd be next. And there'd be no one left to protect you."

I want to make this moment last. Lada isn't looking at me but I can tell she's being sincere. She does care about me. "You don't have to worry about me, Lada," I say, trying to reassure her. She manages a small smile this time but I can tell my words mean little to her. "I mean it. If I've got this 'gift' then I'll be fine—once I learn how to use it."

"You don't understand, Nyla. You consumed a huge amount of malevolent energy today. It's inside of you now. It's a part of who you are."

"Osiris said I converted it somehow."

"Osiris doesn't know what he's talking about! For now, all he can do is speculate. They won't know the extent of your abilities until they run a slew of tests on you. Do you understand what that means?"

"They're not going to turn me into some sort of lab rat. They need me."

Lada nods slowly and crushes the soda can once more. "That's right. Which is why they'll put you back in the deep. And then they'll stand back and wait to see just how much you can stand."

"Roan said I'm valuable to The League. If that's true, why would they let anything bad happen to me?"

Lada presses the heels of her hands into her eyes, blocking me from sight. After a few seconds she pulls her hands away and shakes her head wearily. "I can't help you, Nyla. I wish I could. But what you have inside of you…it's not like anything I've seen before."

It's clear she doesn't mean that in a good way. "But you're my mother," I say. "Whatever's inside of me must have come from you."

Lada shakes her head. "Maybe it skipped a generation…"

"Wait a minute—your mother was like this, too?"

"Not as far as I could tell. But I used to hear stories about my father's mother. They said she was 'eccentric' but maybe she was like us. Like you."

Once again I am reminded that my mother is a stranger to me. I know nothing about her or her family—my relatives. "What was her name?"

"My grandmother? Imaculada."

"You were named after her?"

Lada nods. "It's Portuguese, I think."

Lada piles her trash onto the orange plastic tray, signaling the end of our conversation. "Think about what I said. I'm sure Roan could help you get on the Pill."

"Roan's not my mother," I remind her.

"No, but you should think of her as a big sister. I won't be here forever."

"Meaning?"

"The League is global, Nyla. We go where we're told to go. Marta knows I don't approve of her plans for you. I'll probably be reassigned before too long. That's how The League deals with dissent."

"Is that what you want—to be sent away from me?"

Finally our eyes meet and I see the woman my mother used to be. The woman she was before she joined The League. "If I'd stayed longer, I only would have loved you more," she says softly. "Understand?"

Before I can answer, Lada slides out of the booth and walks away. She slams her tray and everything on it into the trash without looking back at me.

9.

I find my own way back to the apartment. I don't know this neighborhood all that well, but I think there's an art school close by. If I'm right, then that means I'm not that far from home. I need to call Sachi and Cal. I pull my phone out but shove it back in my pocket and decide to call them once I'm in a room with a door. I don't want to start blubbering in the middle of the street.

I take the elevator up to the sixth floor. Lada left the apartment door slightly ajar so I don't knock. I just slip inside, close the door behind me, and head for the room I slept in earlier. I walk in and find Roan standing in front of the dresser, a towel wrapped around her waist. She's combing her long, black hair, which is long enough to cover one of her bare breasts.

I blush and turn away. "Sorry. I should have knocked. I—I thought this was my room."

"It is," she says, totally unfazed. "We're roommates."

I sit on my bed and face the wall to give her some privacy. "Mind if I make a quick call?"

"You can't tell anyone where you are. You know that, right?"

I glance over my shoulder and am relieved to see that Roan is now wearing a t-shirt and plaid pajama pants. It's strange to see her looking so normal after everything that happened in the deep today.

"I know. I just want to let my folks know I'm okay." I touch the screen and pull up a photo I took of Cal and Sachi in Munich at last year's Oktoberfest. We were genuinely happy then—all of us.

Roan watches me while braiding her hair. "I wouldn't do that if I were you."

I touch the screen again and pull up the dial option, hoping she'll find a reason to leave the room. "I won't tell them anything about The League. I just don't want them to worry about me. My stepmother's probably put out an Amber alert already." I grin and try to keep it light but Roan just stands there stone-faced.

Finally she shrugs and says, "Suit yourself," before turning off the lamp in the far corner of the room. Then Roan peels back the beige cover and gets into bed. She turns on her side so that her back is to me. Realizing this is as much privacy as I can expect, I face the wall on my side of the room and press the call icon. The phone barely rings once before Sachi picks up. Her anxious voice confirms what I already know: the past twelve hours have been hell for my folks.

"Nyla? Nyla? Oh, my God—Cal, it's her!"

"Mom—calm down. I'm okay. I just—"

"Where are you? What happened? Are you hurt?"

"I'm fine, Sachi. I just wanted to let you know that—"

Cal gets on the line and starts barking at me in his drill sergeant voice. I know he's worried but I don't need him hollering at me right now. "You come home right this instant, young lady! Do you hear me? I don't know what kind of game you think you're playing—"

"Cal—Cal—would you shut up and listen to me!"

"Hang up, Nyla."

I look over my shoulder and see that Roan is propped up on her elbow, watching me. I want to hang up but I haven't been able to make my parents understand that I'm okay. Roan was right—calling home was a mistake. Sachi's sobbing so loudly that she can't hear a word I'm saying. I need her to hear me but that means raising my voice too.

"Mom, I'm fine—I really am. They're going to train me so I know how to—"

"Nyla, please—*please*, I'm begging you. Just come home. You won't be in any trouble. We just need you to come back to us. Your father's been all over the city looking for you."

Cal finally gets a grip and lowers his voice but only to threaten me. "Don't make me involve the authorities, Nyla. The police have better things to do than chase after ungrateful teenage girls who—"

Suddenly Sachi starts screaming hysterically. "How could you do this to us? How could you just run off and leave me like that?"

"HANG UP!"

Roan reaches across my bed, snatches the phone out of my hand, and ends the call. "I told you not to call them. That isn't your home anymore, Nyla. The League is all the family you've got now."

Roan has more to say but the tears streaming down my face make her reconsider a long lecture. She sighs and tosses my phone onto the bed. "Send a text next time. You can't torture them with the sound of your voice. It's too cruel—for them and for you."

I nod to show that I understand. Then I lie down on the bed, curl myself into a ball, and turn my face into the pillow so Roan won't hear me cry.

Roan stands over me for a moment longer. Then she says wearily, "Get some rest. We've got a full day tomorrow."

I hear the soft click as Roan turns off the lamp on the nightstand between our two beds. Even though she's just a few feet away, I have never felt so alone. I lie awake in the blackness asking myself over and over, *What have I done?*

It's almost noon when I wake the next day. The apartment is eerily quiet. I find Roan sitting alone in the beige kitchen, the only room that feels even a little bit homey. Sunlight streams through the venetian blinds and a thriving plant hangs from a hook in the ceiling.

"Sleeping Beauty wakes at last," Roan says with a smile.

"Where is everyone?"

"At work. Marta's here, of course, but she said to let you sleep in. Want an omelet?"

"Is there coffee?"

"Instant decaf. You okay with that?"

I nod and slump into the empty chair at the table. Right now I need caffeine like I need air. Sachi always warned me away from energy drinks but I could sure use one today. I've slept for more than twelve hours but I still feel bone tired.

The blue flame leaps up as Roan sets a pot of water on to boil. "Why aren't you with the others?" I ask her.

"Marta wanted me to stick around and help you settle in." She watches me for a moment. I'm too tired to tell whether she's genuinely concerned or wary after my debut yesterday. "How do you feel?"

"Beat."

"That's how you look. Don't worry—a hot shower and a hot meal should do the trick. I left some clean towels on your bed."

"Thanks." It will take a couple of minutes for the water to boil. I search for something light to talk about but don't really feel like chatting about the weather with Roan. My head's still full of unanswered questions.

"I've been thinking..."

"Uh oh. Didn't Lada tell you? Thinking's not allowed. Or strongly discouraged, at least."

Roan's smirk gives me the confidence I need to go on. "The energy you're trying to bury in the deep—"

"Mal-N. Malevolent energy."

"Right. How do you know it's evil? I mean, it didn't look evil to me."

"Oh no? How did it look to you?"

I shrug and recall how the energy morphed from butterflies to worms to silver dust to daggers. "Beautiful…in a way."

Roan leans against the kitchen counter and folds her muscular arms across her chest. "Mal-N can take many forms. But it's trapped down there for a reason and for countless generations people like us have been fighting to preserve the balance that favors life."

Her response sounds like something Roan memorized from a book. "So…it's not the energy itself that's the problem. It's how much reaches the surface?"

"That's one way of looking at it. One of our biggest challenges right now is fracking. People want all that cheap natural gas but they don't want to deal with the adverse consequences of drilling so deep. We've got people working to slow things down but it's like the gold rush back in the day."

"You've got people?"

"Organizers, attorneys, journalists. We don't all work underground." Roan turns off the burner and spoons coffee crystals into a mug before filling it with boiling water.

I decline her offer of milk, and take a gulp of bitter black coffee, scalding the roof of my mouth. "So the League's been around for a long time?"

Roan nods. "We even have an archivist. Every culture in every era has had to confront the problem of evil. People think hell is this fiery pit in the belly of the earth and Satan's down there waiting for them with a pitchfork. But evil's a lot more complicated than that."

It spoke to me. I want to say the words aloud but instead I take a second, more cautious sip of coffee and ask, "Are you sure we're winning the battle? I mean, seriously messed up stuff happens every day."

"Suffering is a part of life, Nyla. We're not trying to create some sort of utopia. But would you really want to live in a world filled with more wars? More crime? More senseless violence? The League is all that stands between the world we know—imperfect as it is—and total chaos."

I think back to what Osiris said yesterday about Roan's friend Cairene. I want to ask her why all the war, crime, and senseless violence seem to be committed by men. If they're the problem, what's the solution? Maybe it isn't in the deep after all. Or maybe it is.

"What if—what if we found a way to convert the energy so it wasn't malevolent any more? I mean, that's what I did yesterday, right?"

"We don't know what you did, Nyla. Maybe you changed it—maybe it changed you. You could be a ticking time bomb for all we know. Some new kind of carrier. Mal-N always corrupts its host."

"It didn't corrupt me. It helped me heal you—and Osiris."

"Think you could do that now?"

I look away, knowing all too well that whatever power I had yesterday is long gone. I take another sip of coffee and then order a cheese omelet before heading to the bathroom for a shower. The hot water does perk me up a bit and once I've changed, I find out that Roan's a pretty good cook. She watches me while I eat and before long I find myself telling her about the other adventure I had underground with D and Keem. Roan listens to my story without showing any sign of doubt or disbelief. I wonder what it would take to shock someone who's already seen so much. Then I think about what Lada said last night. Having a big sister might not be such a bad thing after all.

When I reach the end Roan asks, "So this Nuru creature—it went back to its own realm?"

"Sort of. I think a part of her stayed inside of D. He can still feel her sometimes." I fill my mouth with food to give myself time to arrange my next words. "Maybe I'll be that kind of host."

"Maybe." Roan says nothing more until I shove the last bite of toast into my mouth. Then she glances at her watch and says, "There's no rush but when you're ready, Marta wants to talk to you."

Right now I'd really like to crawl back into bed but instead I drain my second cup of coffee and take my dishes over to the sink.

"What's she like?" I ask as I put the plug in the drain and prepare to wash up.

"You'll see," Roan says with a smile that's not entirely reassuring. She gets up to help me but I shoo her away. I clear the table and tell her, "The cook doesn't clean. That was the rule in our house." For just a moment I think of Sachi and Cal. I wonder if my father made waffles for breakfast—our Sunday tradition.

Roan sits back down and fiddles with the antenna of an old portable radio that sits on the windowsill. I get the feeling Roan used to be a smoker. She reminds me of someone who's used to having something to do with her hands. As I wash the dishes Roan sits at the table soaking up the midday sun. I smile as Sam Cooke's voice spills out of the radio. *What a wonderful world this would be.* "My Gran used to love Sam Cooke," I say, almost to myself.

"Can I give you some advice?" Roan asks gently.

I nod over my shoulder and she goes on.

"Try not to think about the past. It's easier if you focus on being here, in this moment. Right now you're washing dishes—focus on that."

"Are you Buddhist?"

Roan laughs. "I'm not anything. But if calling it Buddhism helps you practice mindfulness and nonattachment—go for it. You need a clear head to work in the deep."

I rinse the plate in my hands and set it on the tray with the others. I want to thank Roan for helping me to make sense of this new life but I still feel embarrassed about the scene on the phone last night. "Was it hard for you—letting go of your other life?"

Roan shrugs. "Not really. Most of the people I loved had either died or checked out years ago." She pauses. "There are more things I *don't* miss. I went from being 'white trash' to being one of the best sealers in The League. I've been all over the world. I do work that really matters. That's enough for me."

I fish around in the soapy water until I'm sure there are no more dishes to wash. Then I pull the plug and rinse the suds from my hands.

"Roan?"

Marta's deep voice floats down the hallway, reminding me that we're not alone. Roan goes in search of Marta and returns a moment later with a smile on her face. "You've been summoned."

My hands are clean but I nervously wipe them on my pants just the same. "I feel like I'm about to meet the Queen. Is there anything special I should do?"

Roan puts a hand on my shoulder. "Just be yourself, Nyla." She steers me down the hallway. "Relax. This isn't a test. Marta just wants to get to know you."

"Will you be there too?"

"I can stay, if that's what you want."

"It is. I want you to stay—please."

Roan smiles again and pushes open the door to Marta's room. There is a bulge in the beige carpet that makes it hard to open the door more than a couple of feet. I slip inside and wait for Roan to follow. She gestures for me to sit at the round table in the middle of the room. Overhead is a tacky, stained-glass lampshade from the '70s, which explains the orange glow from last night.

Marta is standing at the window. From behind she looks like somebody's grandmother with her grey hair pulled into an untidy bun and her flowery housedress and faded pink slippers. But when she turns around I see that despite her unkempt appearance, Marta's got the face of a shrewd businesswoman. She doesn't quite smile as she regards me for what feels like ten long minutes. Her grey eyes are startling against her brown skin.

"Welcome," she says at last.

"Nyla would like me to stay," Roan says in a voice that makes it sound like she's asking permission.

Marta nods but says, "So long as you don't interrupt."

Roan parks herself along the beige wall to my right. When I glance over at her she nods at Marta, reminding me to focus.

Marta comes over to the table and pulls out the chair opposite mine. "You look tired."

"Yes, ma'am."

"Please, call me Marta. As you can see, we're an informal organization. Didn't you sleep well?"

"I did—eventually." I resist the urge to look over at Roan. Did she tell Marta about my disastrous attempt to call home?

"Sometimes it takes a while to adjust to a new environment. Unfortunately, the nature of our work requires us to move rather frequently. Just as soon as you get used to one bed you find yourself sleeping in another. Isn't that right, Roan?"

I don't know if Marta can read minds but I appreciate her giving me the opportunity to shift my gaze away from her stern, ageless face. Roan is slouched against the wall. She nods at Marta and then winks at me.

I manage not to giggle, though that's what I do when I'm nervous. "I'm sure I'll be fine by tomorrow," I assure them both.

"I'm glad to hear that," Marta says. "You're joining us at a critical time, Nyla. I believe Osiris has told you we're expecting significant seismic activity over the next few days."

"Yes, ma'am. I mean, yes—he has."

"I won't keep you long since you're tired, but I do want to make clear some of the principles that drive our work. You have a remarkable gift, Nyla, and I'm very pleased that you've agreed to commit yourself to The League. You should know, however, that there are considerable risks involved in the work that we do. And we offer no formal compensation. Your basic needs will be covered, of course, and we'll do everything in our power to keep you safe. But, as I suspect you know, there are forces in this universe that are beyond our control." Marta pauses and looks at me expectantly.

I don't know what to say so I mumble, "Um, yeah."

Marta frowns and I feel my cheeks burn with shame. How is this supposed to work? For a moment I feel resentment toward Lada who left me here without telling me what to do. Roan silently slides further along the wall so that I can see her and Marta at the same time.

"You must indicate that you understand all that I am telling you, Nyla, otherwise your training cannot proceed."

"Sorry." I glance at Roan and see her mouth, "I understand."

"Let's start again," Marta says with a kind smile. "There are forces in this universe that are beyond our control."

"I understand."

"Good. Now, there are some among us who have been blessed with the ability to detect such forces."

I dart my eyes at Roan and she nods back. "I understand," I say once more.

"Such a blessing can feel, at times, like a curse but those gifts must not be squandered. They must be used in defense of all that is good in this world."

I think of the metal embedded in my face and my weary body starts to ache as I sit in this hard, wooden chair. Still I nod and say, "I understand."

"You have greater ability than most, Nyla."

Marta pauses. I open my mouth to give the usual reply but then realize she has something else to say. "Arrogance is our greatest enemy. It will destroy us all. Your gifts must be handled with respect and humility. Joining The League requires each of us to surrender our ego, our ambition, and our attachment to the external world. It can be a lonely sort of life."

I look beyond Marta to the blue sky beyond the window. I think of the phone in my pocket, the many unread messages I will have to delete. I think of Keem and wonder how it would feel to never see him again. I think of D always preparing for the people he loves to walk out on him. I think of how proud I felt when my acceptance letter arrived from Stuyvesant High. Roan is watching me closely from her place along the wall. I need to focus. I force my gaze to return to Marta's face.

"Nyla, do you understand?"

I'm not making any promises. I'm just confirming that the rules are clear. That doesn't mean I have to follow them. I nod heartily and say, "I do, Marta. I understand."

"Good. You are, to date, our youngest recruit. I expect that the break with the outside world will be especially difficult for you. But it must be made, Nyla. You cannot cling to your old life. That would only bring heartache and impotency."

I try to hide my confusion but Marta picks up on it anyway and offers an explanation. "Your gift demands absolute devotion. Without it your power will be diminished. We will do all we can to help you develop your abilities but you cannot have divided loyalties. The League must become your top priority."

"I understand."

"I hope so. Now, do you have any questions for me?"

Where do I begin? I decide to start with Lada. "Is my mother being reassigned?"

"That has not yet been determined. Do you want her to stay?"

I hesitate, once again unsure of the consequences of telling the truth. "I don't know. She says she can't help me. And I know it's hard for her to…watch."

"Lada's attachment to you may become a liability in the deep, though it could also enhance her efficiency. That remains to be seen."

Efficiency? Meaning what—that she'll work harder if she knows my life is at stake too? That's messed up. I don't know if Marta is as heartless as she sounds, but at least she's not sugarcoating anything. "Yesterday I saw the mass suck something out of her—it looked like a bright blue cord. Lada said it had something to do with core energy."

"All matter is composed of energy. When a member of The League falls in the deep, her energy is absorbed by the malevolent mass. It's unclear whether the mass can absorb consciousness—memory, intelligence—but it does seek the particular intuitive abilities of our members."

"Why?"

"That is the source of our power. People like us are highly intuitive, Nyla."

"Intuitive. You don't mean, like, psychic?"

"No, dear. Our success relies upon our ability to detect shifts in energy—minute shifts that happen miles underground. The League needs people who possess a certain sensitivity to changes in the environment. They demonstrate an affinity for processes in the natural world. Roan, for instance, is a sealer because she is able to help solid rock to remember its prior form—the state it was in before the fissure opened, allowing malevolent energy to rise."

It feels weird talking about Roan like she's not here but I know Marta expects me to direct my questions to her. "So…does that mean she could 'help' a piece of paper 'remember' being a tree?"

"Not quite. But I will refer you to Lada on that point. She draws her intuitive power from wood taken from ancient trees."

"Her pole."

Marta nods. "A source object is a kind of…witness. Source objects hold memories of the world as it once was. In a way, our project is one of restoration."

"Will I be given a source object—or do I get to choose my own?" My choice is already made, of course. I resist the urge to reach inside my pocket for the amber ring Keem gave me.

"You may choose your own, but it is not yet clear what your role will be within our organization."

"I thought I'd be a presser—like my mother."

"Tomorrow Roan will take you back into the deep. She'll open a seam and we'll see how you manage in a more controlled environment. Yesterday you were tested rather unexpectedly."

"But I passed the test, right?"

"Yes, but your mother's life was at stake. We need to know what you're capable of when you're not under duress." Marta pauses to examine her ragged cuticles. "May I ask *you* something, Nyla?"

"Sure."

"When you confronted the malevolent mass yesterday why did you choose to consume it? Why didn't you flee? Most people would have."

I shrug. "Everyone keeps telling me I'm different—special somehow. I just felt like there had to be something I could do. Would you have left *your* mother to die?"

"The circumstances were certainly distressing. I suppose I'm wondering how deliberate your actions were. Did you know what you were doing?"

This feels like a trick question. I decide to tell Marta the truth. "No—not exactly. I just had a feeling inside. Maybe it was intuition."

Marta smiles. "Maybe. You look tired, dear. Why don't you go lie down for a while. We can continue our conversation another time."

I glance at Roan. She pushes herself off the wall, which helps me understand that I have been dismissed. I get up and try not to groan as my stiff limbs unfold themselves. I tug at the door but can't manage to open it very far. I look over my shoulder to see if Roan is coming with me.

"I'll be out in a minute," she says, taking my seat at the round table.

I nod and close the door as best I can on my way out. I linger in the hallway but neither woman speaks for several seconds and so I head back to my room. I check my phone. There are a zillion messages from Sachi and Cal, but I skip those and open the latest text from Keem. I think carefully about what I can tell him about what's going on in my life. Fatigue weights my body to the bed and I feel my eyelids starting to close. I have never been this tired before and wonder if I'm coming down with something. I hope not—I want to be in top form when Roan takes me back into the deep tomorrow.

My head falls back against the soft pillow. I bring my phone up close to my face and pull up the photo Nasira took of me and Keem the day I wore his mother's wedding dress. I never saw a definite future for the two of us, but the thought of never seeing Keem again fills me with a kind of sadness I've never felt before. I send him a quick text that is both safe and true: *I miss you.* Then I close my eyes and fall into a deep, dreamless sleep.

10.

I wake in the middle of the night with a hunger so intense it makes me nauseous. Without waking Roan I slip out of the bedroom and creep down the hallway to the kitchen. I take a jar of peanut butter and a loaf of bread out of the fridge but when the sandwich is ready, I find I can't swallow a single bite. My tight, sore throat accepts just a few sips of water and even those make my stomach cramp almost immediately. I double over and rest my forehead on the hard surface of the formica tabletop. It feels as if a heavy hand is pressing down on me, and before long I slide off the chair and onto the floor. I am quietly weeping into the beige linoleum when Liev finds me.

He digs his steel toe boot into my side until I manage to lift my head and look up at him. "Why are you on the floor?"

"I—I fell." I struggle onto my hands and knees and manage to pull myself back onto the chair.

Liev watches me without a trace of emotion in his pale face. Finally he says, "I'll get Lada."

I find the energy to reach out and grab his arm. "No—please. I'm fine. I just need to go back to bed." I place my palm on the table and try to stand but can barely lift my body off the chair. Liev scowls at me but puts his arm around me and lifts me to my feet. "Thank you," I whisper without looking in his face.

Liev half drags me down the hall, kicks open the bedroom door, and dumps me on the bed. Roan wakes up and sees him flinging my limp legs under the covers.

"What the hell? Get off her, you creep!"

Liev makes a sound of disgust—or amusement. "Relax. I found her on the kitchen floor. She's your responsibility, Roan—not mine." He walks out without another word and without closing the bedroom door.

Roan rushes over to the door and scans the hallway to make sure no one else is up. Then she closes the door and stands at the foot of my bed with her hands on her hips. "It's 3am, Nyla!"

I open my mouth to apologize but fatigue overwhelms me, and sleep swallows me up once more. I wake hours later to find the room full of sunshine and Roan seated on the edge of her bed staring at me. She's fully dressed and swings her crossed leg impatiently.

"What time is it?" I ask, holding up a hand to shield my eyes from the bright light.

"Almost eleven."

"What? Why didn't you wake me?"

"I tried. You sleep like the dead." Roan stands and goes over to the door. "I'll be in the kitchen. Come get me when you're ready to get to work."

I drag myself out of bed and hurry down the hall to the bathroom to wash up. I put on some clean clothes and manage not to keep Roan waiting more than fifteen minutes. I feel better than I did at 3am but decline her offer to make me something to eat.

"Nervous?" she asks with a sympathetic smile.

I nod and follow Roan out of the apartment, hoping my energy lasts long enough for me to prove myself in the deep. Somehow just the thought of going back underground makes me feel stronger and more alert.

"Will Lada be there?" I ask as we step into the elevator. I keep my tone casual, though I'm anxious to know the answer. I haven't seen Lada since Saturday night and I'm not sure anyone would actually tell me if she had already been reassigned. Not that I could do much about it if she had.

I sigh with relief when Roan shakes her head. "Lada spent all night in the deep. Marta told her to get a few hours of sleep. The days before a surge are always hectic. We're a little short-staffed so folks are extending their shifts."

We walk out to the street. Roan hails a cab and tells the driver to drop us at Grand Army Plaza. We don't talk during the short drive and I fight to hide my growing excitement. By the time we pull up to the curb I'm grinning from ear to ear and all the fatigue I've been feeling has disappeared.

I have no trouble keeping up with Roan as she sprints across the lanes of traffic that loop around the big arch. It's Monday so the park inside the roundabout isn't very crowded, but there are still a few people eating lunch on the benches by the fountain. As we near the arch, I look ahead and feel my heart leap inside my chest. Before Roan can stop me, I launch myself at Keem and pull his head down so I can cover his mouth with my own.

We pull apart when Roan clears her throat and says, "You've got two minutes, Nyla." Then she walks off before I can thank her.

Keem doesn't seem to notice Roan. He acts like I'm the only person in the plaza. I beam up at him and try not to hear the clock ticking in my head. Two minutes isn't enough but it's all I've got. "I'm so glad you're here."

"Where've you been? I called your house and your dad said you were out of town."

I drop my head, ashamed that I let so much happen in my life without telling Keem. I haven't got time for the whole story so I tease out the most important parts. "Lada told my folks to take me out of the city. Sachi tried to, but—I ran away."

Keem frowns. "Why?"

"Because this is where I belong. With The League, in the deep."

"With your mother."

I nod, grateful that Keem understands. "I'm in training, Keem. I'm learning how to make the world a safer place. Even your dad would approve of that!"

Keem doesn't smile. "School starts in a couple of weeks. Will your training wrap up by then?"

I want to look away but I also want Keem to know I'm telling him the truth. So I focus on his beautiful face and say, "This is more important than school."

Keem says nothing for a long time. He just looks at me like I'm walking away from him. But I'm not walking away. I take his hand in mine so he realizes that I'm still standing there beside him.

"This is what you want?" he asks finally. I nod and he brings his free hand up to caress my face, tracing circles around my new, permanent adornments. "Was that part of your initiation?"

"Nyla!"

I glance over my shoulder and see the impatience stamped on Roan's face. "I can't explain everything now. But I will—I'll tell you everything soon. I promise."

Keem casts a wary glance at Roan. "Can I come with you?"

I shake my head. "I'm breaking the rules now just by talking to you. They're kind of strict and I need to prove that I'm serious about joining their team."

"So what do you have to do—pass some sort of test?"

"Something like that. They know I have potential. I just have to show them that I can stay cool under pressure."

Keem smirks. "You mean you got to keep that wicked temper of yours in check!"

I laugh and give Keem a playful shove before grabbing a fistful of his t-shirt and pulling him close again. "I can do this, Keem."

"I know. You can do anything, Nyla." Keem bends down so that our lips meet again.

Roan finally gets tired of waiting for me and marches up to us with a serious scowl on her face. I untangle my fingers from Keem's and put some space between us. "This is Roan. She's showing me the ropes."

Roan's not interested in introductions. She gives Keem the once over and says, "Get lost, kid. We've got work to do." Before I can object she cuts her eyes at me and says, "Wait for me by the door, Nyla."

I know Roan well enough by now to know that's an order, not a request. I try to apologize to Keem with my eyes as I back away. "I gotta go."

I expect Roan to follow me but she doesn't move. Instead she gets in Keem's face. He's taller than her, of course, but Roan's pretty fierce when she wants to be. "Why are you here? You've got nothing she needs. *Nothing*."

Keem puts on his game face and stares Roan down. "We've been underground before, you know."

Roan tips her head back and laughs in his face. "From what I hear, you outran a couple of ancient ghosts. Think that means you've got what it takes?" She looks at Keem with total contempt. "You have no idea what we're dealing with in the deep. Nyla's got a job to do. She doesn't need any distractions—or dependents."

That strikes a nerve. Keem nearly chokes on the word. "Dependents?"

"That's right—she can't do her job if she has to look out for you."

"I can look out for myself."

"Not down there, you can't. She's beyond you now." Roan finally backs off. "You really care about her?"

"Yeah. I do."

"Then let her go."

Roan walks away before Keem can say anything else. Then she grabs my arm and practically drags me around the corner of the massive arch.

"Hey—you're hurting me!"

Roan slams me up against the hard marble and puts her face an inch away from mine. "One word. I breathe *one word* of this to Marta and you're done. Understand?"

"I—I didn't know he'd be here. Keem's just a friend..."

"Yeah, right. You practically flew into his arms."

I search for words to defend myself but decide it's best to just keep my mouth shut. I didn't set this up but it means a lot that Keem came looking for me. Roan opens the door with her key and shoves me inside. I grip the railing and ease myself down the circular staircase. By the time we don our hard hats and vests and step inside the elevator, I have figured out what I need to say. "I'm sorry, Roan. It won't happen again." Lying is way too easy for me.

Roan slams the metal gate shut and says, "It better not." Then she presses the buttons that send us into the deep.

When we arrive, Roan explains how the test will work. "We'll find a live site and then I'll make an opening to allow a small amount of mal-N to escape."

"And then?"

Roan shrugs. "We'll see what happens. My instructions are to stand back and observe."

"What if—what if this time I can't—"

"Liev's around here somewhere. You'll have a presser and a sealer on standby, but try not to think about that. Just focus on your reaction to the energy. Your first impulse will be the strongest and that should tell us what your role will be."

I nod and take a deep breath to steady my nerves. I follow Roan down the tunnel until we reach the large cavern. Liev is up against the far wall, tracing some kind of pattern on the black rock. He doesn't return Roan's greeting but watches as she leads me over to a section of the cavern where the ground is marked with four pieces of fluorescent pink tape.

Roan touches her amethyst amulet and looks at me. "Ready?"

My heart is racing. I nod and keep my eyes on the ground as Roan places her palms together and then slowly draws them apart. I hear a faint buzz and then a tiny white speck appears at the mouth of the fissure. I crouch down and watch with a blend of fear and fascination as it grows into a perfect pearl. As soon as I pick it up, another white speck appears and quickly forms a second pearl. Within a few seconds both of my hands are full of the small white spheres. They wobble in my palms like soft-boiled eggs.

I think about what Roan said and decide to trust my first impulse. I open my mouth and shove in as many of the shimmering pearls as I can.

I hear Roan gasp but I am ravenous and show no restraint as I gorge myself on the spongy spheres. When I finally pause long enough to glance up at Roan, I see that she's looking at me like I'm scooping maggots into my mouth. Without taking her eyes off me she calls out, "Liev!"

I continue to feed as he makes his way across the cavern. My blood tingles as it skips through my veins. Overjoyed, I laugh despite my full mouth. Spheres dribble out of the corners of my mouth, further disgusting Roan.

"That's enough," she says, but I can't stop. The faster I eat, the faster the energy bubbles surface.

"Move!" Roan barks.

When I don't obey her command, Roan shoves me—hard. Then she claps her hands together and spreads her arms, preparing to seal the fissure.

Almost without thinking, I lunge at Roan and grab hold of her wrists. For a split second our eyes meet. I search deep inside her black pupils until I find the shimmering blue cord. I extract the knowledge I need and then throw her to the ground before turning back to the fissure. I look at my hands and will them to do what only Roan could do a moment ago. The crack widens and pearls bubble up from the rock like a geyser.

"You little bitch!" Roan hisses at me.

I drop to my knees and press my mouth to the source, desperately consuming as much mal-N as I can.

Liev reaches us and helps Roan get to her feet. I see them approaching out of the corner of my eye, but I can't pull myself away from the source. Liev circles around and grabs me from behind. I struggle to free myself but he only tightens his iron grip on my arms. I kick at Roan but she keeps her distance and instead focuses on sealing the rock.

Once she's done, Roan looks at me and say, "You're sick, you know."

Shame forces my eyes away from hers. Roan nods at Liev and he roughly tosses me aside. I turn away from them, wipe at my mouth, and then lick the stray bubbles off my fingers. My heart sinks when I hear Roan say, "We're done here. Check the seal."

Liev drops to one knee and runs his fingers over the ground. "Tight—as always."

Roan accepts the compliment with a nod. Then she turns to me and says, "Let's go."

"But…there's more down there." I know how pathetic I sound, but only mal-N will satisfy the hunger I feel.

"Of course, there's more down there," Roan says impatiently. "But in case you haven't noticed, our job is to *keep* it down there."

I need more. I can't bring myself to say the words out loud but I can tell from the way Roan's looking at me that she knows. I try to ignore the craving inside and search for a way to redeem myself. "So what do we do now—help Liev?"

Roan stalks off, shaking her head and muttering under her breath. I want to find a reason to linger in the deep but it's clear she's ready to go.

When we get back to the apartment, Roan heads straight for Marta's room. She tries to slam the door behind her but the bulge in the carpet denies her that dramatic effect. I stand in the hallway, listening to Roan's frantic report.

"I want to be reassigned."

Marta doesn't seem surprised or concerned by Roan's agitated state. "You're needed here, Roan. You know that."

"Well, I'm not going back down there with her. She's *sick*!"

"You'll do as you're told," Marta says in her deep, calm voice. "Nyla has to learn how to control her gift."

"Gift? She's a freaking addict, Marta. She actually wants it to surface—she *needs* it! You should have seen her, pawing at the rock after I'd closed the seam. It was disgusting."

"Why did you close the seam?"

"What?"

"If she wanted more, why did you deny her?"

I can just imagine the stunned look on Roan's face. Before she can recover, Marta goes on.

"Your job is to monitor her behavior, not make moral judgments."

"What are you talking about, Marta? The League is all *about* morality. We're down there fighting evil, for fuck's sake."

"Resistance is no longer our only option, Roan. I'm surprised you need me to explain that to you."

"So from now on you want us to kick back and let this poor kid do everything? What if the mal-N is drawn to her as much as she's drawn to it? You're putting all of us in danger, Marta."

"Nyla is like…a unicorn. Rare, wild, beautiful. Full of unlimited potential. She's magical, Roan."

I actually hear Roan choking on her shock. "She's not a fucking unicorn! She's a frightened teenage girl. I can't believe you're willing to risk everything we've worked for—everything The League is *supposed* to stand for."

"Like everything else in nature The League must evolve, Roan. Nyla represents our future."

"So what are you going to do, Marta? Toss her back into the deep and use her like a sponge? Let her soak up as much evil as she can stand? You've seen what it does to her."

"It enhances her regenerative abilities, allowing her to heal others with a simple touch. You told me that."

"And then a few hours later she's so drained of energy she can barely stand. Do you even care what you may be putting her through?"

"What Nyla needs exists in abundance in the deep. I'm asking you to keep her satiated, nothing more."

"No."

"Roan..." A warning tone creeps into Marta's voice.

"We'll see what Lada has to say about this," Roan says defiantly.

Marta is resolute. "Lada will do as she's told. As will you."

Roan yanks on the door so hard that she manages to pull it over the bulge in the beige carpet. She storms out of the wide open door but only glances at me before heading for the living room. I run after her.

"Roan, wait—please." She still won't look at me. "Where are you going?"

"You know where." She opens the front door, stomps down the hall, and angrily pounds the elevator button.

"Take me with you."

"No!"

"Please, Roan. I need to see my mother."

"I'm going for Lada now. You stay here. Go in your room and close the door. Don't talk to Marta—just stay the hell away from her. You hear me?"

I do as I'm told and Roan returns in less than an hour, but it feels like an eternity. I jump up from my bed when I hear the front door slam shut. I stick my head out of my bedroom door and see Lada coming down the hall.

"Stay in your room," she says. Her voice isn't angry but her face is grim. I do as I'm told and wait to hear what will happen next. Lada's conversation with Marta isn't filled with shouting. After about twenty minutes there's a knock at my door. Lada sticks her head in and asks, "Can I come in?"

I nod and Lada closes the door behind her before sitting on the edge of my bed. She grips her knees with her hands and takes a deep breath before turning to me. "So."

"So."

"Are you alright?"

I don't know why, but I lose it. I cover my face with my hands and press myself up against the headboard, ashamed to be bawling in front of my mother when I was so strong just a couple of days ago.

Lada slides down the bed and tries to pull my hands away. "It's okay, Nyla."

I pull back from her touch. "It's *not* okay! What's wrong with me? I just wanted to help—I just wanted to be like you."

Lada stares at the plain beige bedspread, searching for an answer. "Your situation is unique, Nyla…"

"Roan can't even look at me. She thinks I'm disgusting!"

"That's not true—Roan cares about you. That's why she came and got me."

"Maybe Marta's right. Maybe you should just leave me down there…" Lada starts to say something but I can't hear her because

I've started sobbing again.

Lada tries to get closer to me but I pull my knees up to my chest and turn away from her.

"Listen to me. Nyla?" She grabs hold of my shoulder and gently turns me around. "Listen to me. You're going to be okay. You are."

I blink back my tears and try to pull myself together. "I'm so sorry," I whisper. "I didn't know it would be this way."

"Don't apologize, sweetheart. This isn't your fault. But you've got to let us handle this, okay? You can't go back into the deep."

"I have to! The mal-N is there and I *need* it."

"I know. And we'll find a way to get it for you. But you can't go back there now—not when we're expecting some sort of quake. It's too dangerous."

"You're going," I say petulantly.

"We're all going—it's our job. And we've got the experience it takes to handle this situation. You don't."

"I want to help. I still *can* help! Can't I?"

"Not if you're unable to control your…urge. We'd be working at cross-purposes—me pressing the mal-N down, you pulling it up. For now I need you to stay here in the apartment with Marta. Okay?"

I nod but without looking Lada in the eye. She lifts my chin and forces me to look into her face. "Promise me, Nyla. Promise me you'll wait here. I'll come back for you—I will. I'm going to take care of you from now on, just like I used to when you were a little girl."

I look my mother in the eye and lie. "I promise." I lie because those two words get me what I've wanted for years. Lada folds me in her arms and holds me close—not like I'm some pathetic freak, but like I'm the daughter she always dreamed of.

11.

Roan and I didn't always get along but she did give me some good advice: *Don't look back.* She told me to let go of the past and simply be in the present moment, and that's what I'm trying to do. It's easier said than done, of course, but I can't change what happened that day in August. New Yorkers were rattled by an earthquake, and then a few days later the city got lashed by the tail end of Hurricane Irene. The Afro-punk Festival was canceled and in the midst of that chaos my life changed forever.

I promised Lada I would stay in the apartment but when I woke up that morning, I knew I'd have to return to the deep. Roan was right—I *was* like an addict and the craving was so strong it couldn't be ignored. I spent a few hours online, clearing out my inbox, and then in the afternoon the earthquake hit. For half a minute I felt the city shake and I just *knew* a wave of mal-N was rising in the deep. I needed it. There's not much more I can say.

I shouldn't have, but I called Keem. Getting past Marta wasn't a problem—in a way I think she wanted me to go back to the deep. Maybe I could have asked her for the key to the door in the arch, but I didn't have the nerve. Instead I called the strongest person I knew and Keem met me at Grand Army Plaza within half an hour. D was with him, which didn't surprise me. Maybe Nuru was right. Maybe the three of us really are bound to one another.

D and I kept watch while Keem broke down the door on the side of the arch. I wanted them to leave at that point but they're my friends—they could tell something was wrong with me and they weren't about to leave me on my own. So all three of us went into the deep. We were in such a rush that we didn't even bother with the hardhats and fluorescent vests. I should have taken better care of them but I couldn't focus on anything else at the moment. Plus they had each other—and D still had Nuru somewhere inside of him. I just hoped that would be enough to keep them safe.

When we stepped out of the elevator we could tell that something was wrong. We could hear yelling in the distance and so we headed down the tunnel in the direction of the noise. Except for Marta, the apartment had been empty so I knew that meant all hands were on deck. Keem and D thought we were searching for the others but I was really looking for a chance to slip away. I didn't want my friends to see me feed. I didn't want them to know what I'd become. How could I ever explain myself? I told Keem I was fighting evil but the truth was that mal-N was the one thing I needed above everything—and everyone—else.

When we reached the main cavern D asked, "Which way?"

Frantic voices were bouncing off the walls, making it hard to pinpoint the source. I could hear Osiris barking commands and it sounded like the team of Roan, Lada, and Liev was close to success. I had to reach them before they closed the seam and trapped the mal-N beyond my reach. So when D and Keem looked to me for directions I deliberately steered them down the wrong tunnel.

"Are you sure?" Keem asked. "It sounds like everyone's over there."

I assured him it was just an acoustic trick and then pulled back as he and D raced down the tunnel. When they finally realized I wasn't behind them, it was too late. I had vanished into the darkness.

12.

I knew something was wrong even before the earthquake hit. On Monday night I went to bed early and told Mrs. Martin I wasn't feeling well so she'd let me stay home from math camp the next day. I couldn't see Nuru's light but I felt her stirring inside of me—she seemed restless, which is how I knew I needed to be ready for something big. When Keem called that afternoon I was already halfway out the door. I knew it was about Nyla—it had to be. Keem never sounded like that unless something was up between the two of them. I didn't ask questions—we agreed to meet at the library and then we made our way over to the big arch at Grand Army Plaza.

Keem had told me about the silver implants in Nyla's face but it was still hard not to stare when I saw them for myself. She was waiting for us on a bench by the Neptune fountain, staring intently at the merman as if sound and not water were pouring out of the conch shell held to his mouth.

"Thanks for doing this, you guys." Nyla was smiling but she didn't look so good.

"How'd you get locked out?" I asked. "Aren't you supposed to have a guide?"

Nyla looked away, which is how I knew she was about to lie. "Osiris is busy and…Lada doesn't want me down there today. She thinks I'm not ready."

"Are you?" asked Keem. "I mean, your training just started, right? And that earthquake must have stirred things up down there."

Nyla bit her lip and measured her words carefully. I couldn't tell if she didn't trust us or if she didn't trust herself.

"The League was expecting a surge. They've known about the earthquake for weeks now. I am new to all this but the truth is, I can do things they can't."

"What kind of things can you do?" I asked. Nyla pressed her lips together. I could tell she was irritated but she was trying not to bite my head off.

"I have a kind of…immunity."

I looked at the dark circles under Nyla's eyes and the ashen tone of her skin. "Immunity to what?"

Nyla sighed impatiently. "I don't have time to explain everything, D! Let's just say I can tolerate exposure to the things that they fear. I'm just different that way."

I could tell Keem wasn't buying her story either but he didn't know how to say no to Nyla. We followed her over to the marble arch, swallowing the questions we knew Nyla didn't want to answer.

"Listen, you guys, I know things have been weird lately and I know you're worried about me." Nyla paused and when she looked at me I thought I saw real regret in her eyes. "I'm sorry to drag you into this but I just really need to get down there."

Keem sized up the door, which had no knob and was in serious need of a fresh coat of paint. I watched as he scanned the plaza for cops. There weren't any in sight—the earthquake must have given them something better to do than stop and frisk teens.

Keem gave the door a light kick to test its strength. "You know we're coming with you, right?"

Anger flared in Nyla's eyes but she pressed her lips together once more and weighed her options. "It's against the rules," she said half-heartedly.

Keem smiled, knowing Nyla couldn't refuse if she wanted our help. "Good thing you're an expert at *breaking* the rules."

Nyla laughed in spite of herself. "Think you can *break* down this door? I tried picking the lock earlier but..."

Keem pressed his shoulder into the small door. "Watch out," he said, taking a step back himself. Then he raised his long leg and kicked the door. It rattled but didn't open. His second try sent the door flying inward.

Nyla's face lit up with joy and she stopped to give Keem a quick peck on the cheek before rushing inside. We followed her down the spiral staircase and into the elevator. Nyla took a deep breath and then punched the buttons on the panel slowly and deliberately as if trying to remember a code. "Come on," she muttered anxiously under her breath. For a moment nothing happened. Then the elevator car bounced a couple of times and dropped us into the deep.

I guess we should have known Nyla was going to ditch us. All she really needed was access and once Keem kicked down the door, Nyla had no more use for us. But we didn't know then what she was looking for—or why. She needed our help and we gave it to her because that's what friends do. If Nyla had told us the truth we still would have helped her. But she didn't trust us, and that meant we had to discover the truth for ourselves.

As soon as we stepped off the elevator I felt Nuru moving from my chest to my right hand. Her light guided us down the dark tunnel and into the same large cavern we'd been in before. Nyla sent us down another tunnel but Nuru knew something was wrong. Her light dimmed until we could hardly see where we were going. And that's when we realized Nyla was gone.

Keem freaked out and started calling her name. I reached out in the blackness until my fingers touched the tunnel wall. Then I turned around and started heading back in the direction we'd come. After a few steps Nuru's light returned and we hurried back to the cavern.

Nyla wasn't there but Keem kept hollering her name.

"Knock it off, Keem!"

"Nyla needs our help, D! Someone—or something—took her!"

I sighed and wondered if love really does make you blind. "She ditched us on purpose, Keem."

Keem looked at me like I was crazy. "Why would she do that?"

I held up my hand to silence him. We heard angry voices coming from another tunnel but just as we headed in that direction, the ground shook beneath our feet and we had to press ourselves against the wall as a huge chunk of rock crashed down from above. I thought it must have been an aftershock but when the rumbling stopped, the voices got louder—and this time they were all calling Nyla's name. Keem took off and I raced after him toward the flickering red light at the far end of the tunnel.

We weren't prepared for what we saw when we reached the next cavern. The first thing we noticed was that Nyla wasn't the one who need our help. Osiris was clinging to the edge of a huge crater that seemed to have opened in the center of the cavern floor. Nyla stood just a few feet away, dangerously close to the edge. Her gaze was fixed on something far below and she didn't even seem to notice that Osiris was struggling to pull himself up. Lada and two others—including the guy who snatched me—were trapped on the far side of the gaping hole. They were screaming at Nyla but she didn't even seem to hear them.

In the midst of all that chaos Nyla just stood there transfixed as a wave of red lava rose from the depths. Everyone else was freaking out but Nyla looked—ecstatic.

Keem rushed over to Osiris and grabbed hold of his arm.

Osiris looked over his shoulder at the red mass rising from below. "The glasses—take the glasses!" he hissed.

"What?"

But before Osiris could answer something below grabbed hold of him and he vanished from sight. Keem dove for Osiris and I threw my weight over his legs to keep Keem from going over the edge too.

Lada was screaming, "Nyla—stop! Please, stop!"

But Nyla was oblivious to everything except the rising red mass, and I finally understood that she was controlling it—calling it up from the deep.

"Hold on, man! Hold on!" Keem struggled to hold onto Osiris but finally he had to let go. When Keem pulled back from the crater's edge he was holding the dark cataract glasses in his hand. He had a look of horror on his face and he was trembling. I helped Keem get up and pulled him further away from the murderous red mass. He reached out his arm to bring Nyla along, too, but I stopped him.

"What's she doing?" he asked, finally understanding that the Nyla we knew was gone.

Before I could even try to answer that question Nyla extended both her arms and, with her palms facing upward, slowly raised her hands. The red mass in the crater thinned and reared up like a giant wave about to crest. It towered over Nyla, trembling with rage—or anticipation. Nyla gazed up at it, the joy in her face replaced with a look of grim determination.

Lada and her colleagues were frantically trying to reach Nyla, though I'm not sure what they could have done to prevent what happened next. While the others inched their way along the narrow ledge on the cavern wall, Lada took a few steps back and then used her wooden pole to vault over the crater. She landed close to the crater's edge and very nearly lost her balance and fell in, but still Nyla paid no attention. Instead she spread out her arms as if to embrace the serpent-shaped mass. Nyla opened her mouth and whispered, "Come."

The mass began to weave as if it really was a snake and then it dashed at Nyla, winding itself around her body several times. Nyla simply laughed and flung her hands up toward the roof of the cavern.

The red snake dissolved into what looked like a million rose petals and then reformed as a solid red column. The air became electric as the red mass fought against the rigid form Nyla imposed upon it.

Lada inched toward Nyla, her pole extended before her. "Push it down, Nyla. You can do it. Send it back down where it belongs." Lada kept her eyes on Nyla but quietly summoned her companions. "Liev, Roan—get ready to close this up."

The woman named Roan crept past me and Keem. "She won't let it go, Lada. She *can't*—you know that."

"She can and she will," Lada replied, every bit as determined as her daughter. Then to Nyla she said, "Sweetheart, I need you to listen to me. We're going to do this together, okay? I want you to let it go, Nyla. Let it go and I'll do the rest. Okay?"

Nyla kept her arms up, fixing the mass in place. "It's mine." The words were said softly, without defiance, but Lada became stern.

"Let it go, Nyla. If you ever want to become one of us, you've got to let it go. *Now*."

Finally Nyla turned to face her mother. In that same soft voice she said, "No." Then she flung her arms behind her back, opened her mouth wide, and began to inhale the red mass.

"Push her in!"

Lada spun around and aimed her pole at Liev's throat. "No!"

He froze but didn't back down. "Push her in, Roan! She'll take the mal-N with her and then we can close the seam."

But the white girl faltered and by the time she made a decisive move toward Nyla, Keem stood in her way. While Lada kept Liev at bay, Keem shielded Nyla from Roan. And all the while Nyla *fed*. She gorged herself on the seething red mass until it disappeared completely.

Nyla began to burn—her skin, her hair, her clothing, everything turned a livid shade of red. Only the peaceful look on Nyla's face assured us she wasn't in pain. Then, without looking at any of us, she opened her arms, lifted herself into the air, and *flew* over to the far side of the crater. Nyla landed perilously close to its edge, lowered her arms, and gazed down into the abyss.

We felt a slight tremor beneath our feet and heard a low buzz as a second wave of energy began to build in the deep.

Liev took advantage of Lada's distracted state and swatted the pole away from his face. "Damn it, Lada! You just cost us our best chance to make this right. Now your demon daughter is calling up more!"

Lada made one last plea. "Nyla! Nyla, *please*. You've had enough!"

Nyla raised her eyes and looked at us. Then she held out her palm and touched the crackling air as if there were a sheet of glass separating her from us. Nyla took a couple of seconds to look each of us in the eye, and then with a tap of each fingertip she knocked all five of us back, one by one, until we were sprawled on the floor of the tunnel. Nyla took a longer moment to focus on Roan and then she pressed her palms together, closing the mouth of the tunnel.

"NO!" Lada screamed. She jumped up and beat against the wall with her fists. "Nyla! NYLA!"

Roan pulled herself up and tried to drag Lada away from the wall. "We need to get out of here."

"What about Nyla?" I asked.

"She's made her choice," Liev said in that infuriatingly flat voice.

"Asshole," Keem muttered under his breath. "I'm not going anywhere without Nyla."

Roan looked at him with disdain. "I told you before—she's beyond you, kid."

Before Keem could respond Lada spun around and grabbed Roan by the shoulders. "Open it!"

"What?"

"Nyla borrowed your power as a sealer but you can reverse what she's done! We need to get back inside the cavern."

Roan peeled Lada's fingers off her shoulders and backed away, shaking her head. "We have to leave her, Lada. She *wants* us to leave her."

Lada lunged at Roan and grabbed the purple amulet hanging from her neck. "OPEN IT!"

Roan looked straight into Lada's eyes and for a moment it seemed like she was going to obey. Then Lada pulled back a bit and Roan summoned the strength she needed to fling the older woman off. Lada hit the wall of the tunnel and sank to the ground with a grunt of pain.

Roan tucked the amulet back inside her shirt. "I'm done here," she said, casting a contemptuous glance at Lada. Then she turned and walked away without looking back.

Keem helped Lada get to her feet. "What do we do now?"

Lada turned to Liev. "Can you find a fault in this wall?"

Liev narrowed his eyes and studied Lada for a moment. Finally he asked, "Are you sure this is what you want?"

Lada opened her mouth to respond but a sob escaped instead. Choking on emotion, Lada cleared her throat and tried again. "She's my child, Liev. I promised I'd never leave her again."

Liev gave a slight nod and placed his palms on the wall. He closed his cold, blue eyes and began moving his hands across the uneven surface.

Lada took a moment to flick the tears from her eyes and then she turned to me and Keem. "You should go now. If you hurry, you can catch Roan and ride up to the surface with her."

Keem gave me a light shove. "Go on, D."

"What about you?" I asked.

"I'm staying," he replied grimly.

"So am I, then," I said. "Nyla stayed and helped me when she could have walked away."

Liev finally found what he was looking for. "Here," he said, pointing to a place on the wall that was about two feet off the ground. Keem and I watched as Liev placed his hand on Lada's shoulder. "Goodbye, friend," he said before disappearing down the dark tunnel.

Lada focused on her target. "Stand back," she warned.

Keem and I did as we were told. Lada pressed one end of her wooden pole against the spot on the wall. Then she closed her eyes and focused all her energy on the invisible fault until sweat began pouring down her face. The fault developed into a crack and the wall slowly began to pull apart but then Lada had to stop to catch her breath. Keem and I stood by, wishing we could help. I held my hand high, providing light, while Keem anxiously paced before the wall, desperate to get back to Nyla.

After just a minute's rest, Lada took up her pole and tried again. Tears mingled with sweat as she held her pole to the wall and groaned with exertion until the crack widened enough to form a narrow triangular opening.

Lada fell back against the tunnel wall, panting heavily. Keem rushed forward and tried to squeeze through the small break in the wall. It was a tight fit, but he wiggled his way through and I followed behind him. Lada pushed her pole through the opening before squeezing herself into the cavern.

We cautiously approached the edge of the abyss and scanned the cavern but saw no sign of life.

"Nyla!" Keem's desperate voice ricocheted off the walls and swirled down the abyss like water down a drain.

Lada touched his arm to stop him from hollering again. "Listen," she whispered in the eerie silence.

At first we heard nothing. But then we heard—or felt—a soft hum coming from above. We looked up and spotted a star shining on the roof of the cavern. It grew larger as it descended. It was Nyla.

"Stay behind me," Lada said, her pole extended before her.

"Nyla wouldn't hurt us," Keem insisted, stepping out to greet her as she approached. He tilted his face up and drank in the silvery light coming off Nyla's body.

Lada reached out a hand and pulled Keem back. "She's not herself. Right now Nyla's full of energy—malevolent energy."

"She isn't evil," I said, drawing closer to Keem.

Nyla continued to descend until she was level with us. She hung in the black air over the abyss, beyond our reach.

"Nyla?" My voice sounded small and insignificant.

"You shouldn't be here," she said, looking from me to Keem. "This isn't where you belong."

Her voice had an odd metallic ring to it but it was still gentle. It still sounded like Nyla.

Lada joined us at the edge of the abyss. "Have you had enough?"

Nyla shook her head and said, "There will never be enough." Her voice held more certainty than sadness.

"It's time to go, Nyla. We're here to take you home." Keem beckoned her with his hand but Nyla didn't move. She just looked at him and said, "I am home."

Keem frowned, not sure what to say next. He turned to Lada who took a deep breath and tried again. "Nyla, please come with us. We'll find a way to get you what you need—I promise."

"There is no way."

Another mild aftershock rumbled through the deep, sending loose rocks rolling into the abyss. Lada's voice wobbled as her hope grew thin. "It isn't safe for you to stay down here alone."

"I'm not afraid."

Lada shrugged helplessly, unable to come up with any more reasons. Suddenly she yelled, "I'm not leaving you!"

It was hard to tell with such bright light radiating off her body, but I thought I saw Nyla smile. She drew closer to me and Keem and said, "Take care of each other."

Then she drifted toward Lada and held out her hand. "Ready?"

Lada wiped her eyes and set her pole down on the ground. Then she took Nyla's hand and stepped up into the air. Nyla wrapped her mother in a tender embrace and together they dropped into the abyss like a falling star.

AFTER

13.

For days I couldn't eat or sleep. I couldn't even pray.

When I finally got home that evening I went straight to my room. I put Lada's stick and Osiris' glasses in my closet, and then I fell into bed, put a pillow over my head, and tried to forget everything I'd just seen. I wanted to turn back time, to undo what Nyla had done. But time just kept moving forward. I knew because every few hours I heard the call to prayer.

Normally I would get up, perform my ablutions, and then join my father in the dining room. We would lay out our mats and pray side by side while my mother and sister did the same in the living room. But losing Nyla did something to me. When I left the deep my limbs felt like lead, and once I fell into my bed I wasn't sure I could get up again—even if I wanted to. And I didn't want to. I didn't want to think about a future without her.

It was my sister who reminded me that faith is a ladder. Nasira put my hands on the bottom rung and I slowly began to climb.

I'd been in bed for almost two days when I heard a soft knock on the door. Nasira stuck her head into the room. She was wearing her headscarf.

"Can I come in?"

I didn't say anything. I didn't have to. Nasira closed the door behind her and crawled into bed beside me. When she gently pulled the pillow off my face I turned toward the wall. Nasira put her hand on my shoulder and said, "It's Nyla, isn't it."

When I nodded, Nasira asked, "Where is she, Keem? Her father keeps calling, making all kinds of accusations. What happened?"

I needed to say it out loud to know that it was true. "She fell," I whispered.

"Fell? Is she okay?"

I shook my head. "She's not okay. She's gone."

The last word barely made it out of my mouth before I started to howl with grief. Nasira pulled me close to her and held me tight. I wept as she rocked me and when I finally grew quiet again, Nasira said, "I wish I knew what to say, Keem. Ma would recite one of Tagore's poems to make you feel better but I can't think of one that would help right now."

I closed my eyes and pictured Nyla hovering above the chasm, taking her mother with her and leaving me behind. Then the vision disappeared and in its place I saw golden words burning through the gloom of the deep. I heard my own mother's voice struggling to change Bengali words into English so that we could understand the poetry she loved so much. Ma finally bought us a book with English translations of Tagore's work and we used to memorize poems to recite on special occasions.

"'*I have come to the brink of eternity*,'" I whispered. Within seconds Nasira began reciting the rest of the poem.

> In desperate hope I go and search for her
> in all the corners of my room;
> I find her not.
>
> My house is small
> and what once has gone from it can never be regained.

I summon the words of the next verse and say them aloud with my sister.

But infinite is thy mansion, my lord,
and seeking her I have to come to thy door…

I stopped and just listened as Nasira finished the poem. She pressed her lips against my forehead and then left me to sleep. I woke when I next heard the call to prayer coming from the loudspeaker on the nearby mosque. I got up, washed myself, and prepared to pray.

My inbox was overflowing by the time I went back online but I immediately zeroed in on the message from Nyla. It arrived the same day Nyla fell in the deep—she must have sent it before we met at the fountain for the last time.

Keem,

I don't know when I'll see you again and I know I'm a coward for not saying this to your face, but I've never cared about anyone like I care about you. So I hope you can understand how hard this is for me. I've been given this amazing opportunity and I truly believe this is my destiny. Please don't look for me. I'll surface when I can. And no matter what happens, I'll always keep you in my heart.

Love,

Nyla

I read it over and over—at least a hundred times. I couldn't figure out whether the message had been written on the day of the earthquake or earlier. Did she know what was going to happen? Did she plan for us to watch her die? The Nyla I knew wasn't that heartless, but the Nyla I knew is gone.

Months later—after Nasira left for college, after Nyla's dad stopped threatening to have me arrested, and after I tore my ACL in the season opener against Lincoln—I got a text from an unknown number. I almost erased it, thinking it was some sort of scam, but something told me to read it first.

> JSYN I@M OK. RU? PLS 4GIVE ME. I@M SORRY 4 EVRYTHNG. FWIW ILU. BFN.

I don't know where she is or what she's become, but I know now that Nyla's *alive*.

DISCUSSION QUESTIONS

- Nyla keeps a list of all the guys she admires. Make your own List of Good Guys. Which qualities must a person possess in order to earn your trust and/or respect?
- Learn more about the ancient Egyptian myth of Isis and Osiris. Research three other goddesses and pick your favorite one. What strengths or special abilities does she possess? Are female figures worshipped in contemporary religions?
- Sade tries to commit suicide after her boyfriend posts private video footage online. If you were Sade's best friend, what advice would you give her on handling the "sexting" scandal?
- Nyla tells D that being an outsider is a good thing, yet she also struggles to feel at home in Brooklyn. Make a list comparing the advantages and disadvantages of being different than others. What does it mean to belong?
- For ten years Nyla has wondered why her mother walked out on their family. Pretend you are Lada. Write a letter to leave behind for Nyla explaining why you feel it is best to leave. Describe the life you want for your daughter and the world you hope to create by working with The League.
- Read "Poem about My Rights" by June Jordan and "Brink of Eternity" by Rabindranath Tagore. Why do these poems seem to comfort Nyla and Keem? What is your favorite poem?
- Write the first chapter of the next book in this trilogy. Where is Nyla? Will D and Keem see her again? How has her experience in the deep changed her?

ACKNOWLEDGMENTS

"Are you sure you're...*fully* human?"

I woke up hearing those words one morning in 2011. I had almost finished writing *Ship of Souls*, and I instantly knew that the second book in the trilogy would be about Nyla. How would she answer that question? *Was* she fully human? A few days later I was walking up Flatbush Avenue on my way to the Brooklyn Public Library when I saw what looked like an elevator near the entrance to Prospect Park. The modern-looking structure turned out to be a new public toilet, but the idea still lodged in my mind. What if you could drop miles beneath Brooklyn—and what would lure Nyla into the deep? Her long-lost mother, of course.

I didn't plan to self-publish *The Deep* but when I finished the book in March 2013, its publication took on a new level of urgency. Every writer wants to see her work in print, but there was something about this book that demanded immediate attention. I felt sure that there was a teenage girl somewhere in the world who needed this book *yesterday*. I never found anything like *The Deep* when I was scouring the shelves of my public library as a teenager, but it's a story that might have changed my world—or at least my perception of myself. Black girls don't often get to see themselves having magical powers and leading others on fabulous adventures. And so when I received an offer to have *The Deep* published in 2015, I decided this book simply couldn't wait that long.

Self-publishing a book is no small endeavor and I am grateful for all the help I received at each stage of the process. Every year I visit dozens of schools and the students I meet often ask me to tell them about my next project. Their questions force me to weave the loose threads dangling in my imagination into a solid piece of cloth, and so

I thank all the young readers I've met for their enthusiasm and anticipation. It helps to know that my characters are loved, missed, and very much alive in readers' minds.

I thank my friend Kate and my cousin Bethany who are almost always my first readers and kindest critics. I thank John Jennings for producing such a stunning image of Nyla. My friend Stefanie turned John's art into a beautiful cover, and Shadra Strickland connected me with illustrator Ian Moore and Nadirah Iman whose combined talents created the book trailer.

Librarians are an author's best friend for many reasons, not the least of which is help with research. When I needed to confirm facts about Nyla's life on base in Kaiserslautern, I emailed a library there and immediately got a response from Shawn Friend-Begin at Rheinland-Pfalz Libraries. She kindly answered my questions and provided links to further information. When I needed help with aspects of Bangladeshi culture I turned to several women who generously provided advice and assistance; I thank Sabiha, Rifat Salam, and Fariba Salma Alam for sharing their cultural knowledge with me.

Last but not least, I thank my beloved borough for endlessly nourishing my imagination. I am drawn over and over to the magnificent library at Grand Army Plaza—those dazzling, golden images on its façade greeted me when I first arrived back in 1993, and the Brooklyn Public Library has been a sanctuary and source of inspiration ever since. My love for Brooklyn makes so many things seem possible—I always believed I would experience magic here and I have. For that I will always be grateful.

ABOUT THE AUTHOR

Born in Canada, Zetta Elliott moved to the US in 1994 to pursue her PhD in American Studies at NYU. Her poetry has been published in several anthologies, and her plays have been staged in New York, Chicago, and Cleveland. Her essays have appeared in *Horn Book Magazine*, *School Library Journal*, and *Hunger Mountain*. She is the author of three other books for young readers: *Bird* (2008), *A Wish After Midnight* (2010), and *Ship of Souls* (2012). Her short story, "Sweet Sixteen," was published in *Cornered: 14 Stories of Bullying and Defiance* in 2012. Zetta Elliott is Assistant Professor of Ethnic Studies at Borough of Manhattan Community College and currently lives in Brooklyn.

Contact the author at info@zettaelliott.com

ALSO BY

Zetta Elliott

Ship of Souls

A Booklist 2012 Top Ten Sci-Fi/Fantasy Youth Title

★ "Urban fantasies are nothing rare, but few mesh gritty realism with poetic mysticism so convincingly. By turns sad, joyful, frightening, funny, and inspirational, Elliott's second novel is a marvel of tone and setting."
– Daniel Kraus, *Booklist*

"This succinct tale brings well-researched historical background to a compelling urban fantasy. . .a suspenseful story that will leave readers feeling inspired."
– *School Library Journal*

A Wish After Midnight

"Although there is plenty of history embedded in the novel, *A Wish After Midnight* is written with a lyrical grace that many authors of what passes for adult literature would envy."
– Paula L. Woods, *The Defenders Online*

"Zetta Elliott's time travel novel *A Wish After Midnight* is a bit of a revelation. . . . It's vivid, violent and impressive history."
– Colleen Mondor, *Bookslut*

Bird

★ "With unusual depth and raw conviction, Elliott's child-centered narrative excels in this debut." – *Kirkus Reviews*

Made in the USA
Charleston, SC
03 December 2013